QATARI VOICES

A CELEBRATION *of* NEW WRITERS

QATARI VOICES

A CELEBRATION *of* NEW WRITERS

Edited by
Carol Henderson
and
Mohanalakshmi Rajakumar

Published by
Bloomsbury Qatar Foundation Publishing
Qatar Founday
Villa 3, Education City
PO Box 5825
Doha, Qatar
www.bqfp.com.qa

First edition 2010
Reprinted 2012

2 3 4 5 6 7 8 9 10

ISBN 978-9-992-14225-7

Cover by Tarek Dibsi
Cover photos by Natacha Fares &
www.amandadillonphotography.com

The texts by the following authors were previously published in *Qatar Narratives* (2008): Noof Al Khalifa, Rooda Hassan Al Neama, Hissa Faraj Al Marri, Kholoud Saleh, Noura Abdulaziz Al Suwaidi, Nofe Khalid Al Suwaidi, Noora Al Mannai, Al Jazzy Abdullah Al Margahi, Nadya Al Awainati
The texts by the following authors were previously published in *Qatar: Then and Now* (2009): Saad Rashid Al Matwi, Mohammed Fehaid Al Marri, Shaikha Daoud Al Shokri, Amna Abdulaziz Jassim Hamad Al Thani, Buthayna Mohammed Al Madhadi, Fatma bint Nasser K A Al Dosari, Mohammed Jabor Al Kubaisi, Mashaael Salman Rashid, Shaikha Yacoub Al Kuwari, Maryam Ahmad Al Subaiey, Mohammed M Al Khater, Aljohara Yaqoub Al Jefairi

Printed in Great Britain by Clays Ltd, St. Ives Plc, Bungay, Suffolk

Dedication

To those in Qatar who have stories to tell: whether university staff, students or other writers, both nationals and expatriates. It is always a brave act to sit down and let one's thoughts emerge on the page. It's even braver to share those narratives with others, perhaps more so in a small community. We dedicate this book to all those who have shared their stories and to the stories waiting to be written.

Contents

About the Editors

MOHANALAKSHMI RAJAKUMAR is a writer and educator based in Qatar. She is the creator of *Qatar Narratives*, a series of non-fiction books on Qatar. Dr Rajakumar has written several novels and numerous short stories, essays and scholarly pieces, including *Haram in the Harem* (Peter Lang, 2009). Her latest book, *Hip Hop Dance in America* (Greenwood Press, 2012), explores the origins of hip hop culture.

CAROL HENDERSON is a writer, editor and teacher who leads writing groups and works one-on-one as a writing coach and editor. She teaches in the US, Europe and the Middle East and writes for newspapers and magazines. Henderson has edited several memoirs and essay collections, most recently *Wide Open Spaces: Call Stories* (Circle Books, 2011). She is the author of *Losing Malcolm: A Mother's Journey Through Grief* (University Press of Mississippi, 2001) and *Farther Along: The Writing Journey of Thirteen Bereaved Mothers* (Willowdell Books, 2012).

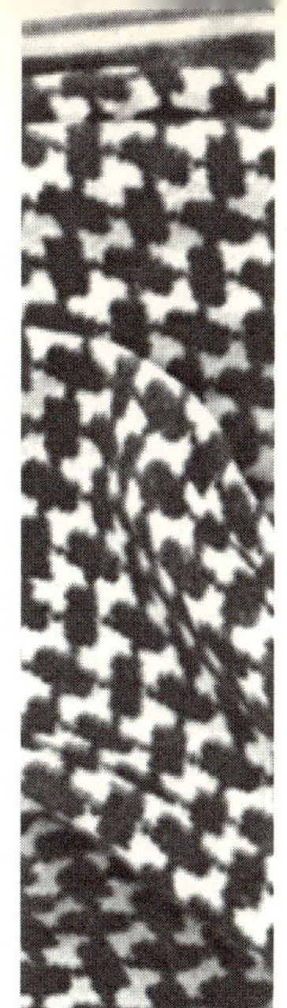

Introduction

"It is really hard to be lonely very long
in a world of words. Even if you don't
have friends somewhere, you still have
language, and it will find you and
wrap its little syllables around you and
suddenly there will be a story to live in."

Naomi Shihab Nye

THE PERSONAL ESSAY has been a thriving writing form for over two thousand years, inviting the reader to eavesdrop on the writer's mind as it meanders on a given topic or issue. A good essayist, like a good writer in any genre, seeks to cultivate an engaging voice, illuminate through concrete example, and transport the reader from an individual to a universal perspective. For aspiring writers in Qatar, the essay has proven to be a powerful vehicle for self-expression and dialogue in the public sphere.

Over the past four years, we have worked with writers across Qatar, encouraging them to express and hone their thoughts within the essay form. This collection, first presented within the *Qatar Narratives* anthology series, features essays by young Qataris who, in these pages and their own words, grapple with the stunning cultural shifts and break-neck speed of change within their culture.

The Editors: A Personal View, or How This Project Came About

The two of us first met in 2006, in the United States, where we were both involved in an intensive writing residency – Mohana as participant, Carol as program director and co-leader. During the week we came to realize that both of us believed strongly in a teaching process that empowers writers to share their truths aloud, uncensored, and in print. Standing in the residence hall doorway late one night after a day of writing, Carol told Mohana, "If you ever need any writing teachers in Qatar, contact me."

Later that year Mohana, then an educational consultant at Qatar University, did just that, inviting Carol to teach a series of writing workshops in Qatar at Education City and Qatar

University, in March 2007, as an experiment to gauge student interest in writing. The workshops during this trial period were well-attended and the students enthusiastic. "We want more of these!" students said again and again.

The American Embassy in Qatar, a partial sponsor for Carol's first trip, invited us to apply for a Middle East Partnership Initiative (MEPI) grant; the purpose of these grants is to build understanding and support cultural awareness through 'soft diplomacy'.

With the grant, and the support of Qatar University, we were able to offer six weeks of writing workshops to female students and staff, focusing on cultivating spontaneity and comfort with writing and thinking in English. Another goal was to encourage the participants to form opinions, without being reticent about communicating those opinions effectively and persuasively in print.

We also offered individual coaching and editing sessions as the budding writers began to refine and further develop their ideas into essays.

Process Writing: The Workshops

The workshop met for six weeks in early 2008. From day one, the students wrote – as soon as they sat down at the large table around which we always met. We started every session with the same writing prompt: "What matters?" Or restated: "What are you *carrying right now*: in your handbag, your heart, your memory, on your shoulders?" Or: "What's in front of you?" In effect, we were inviting everyone at each session to respond to: "What's on your mind, right now?"

This form of writing in response to a prompt is called 'free writing', an approach pioneered by writing authority Peter Elbow (*Writing Without Teachers*) and further developed by Julia Cameron (*The Artist's Way*). When free writing, the writer allows thoughts to spill across the paper, without knowing beforehand where each one will lead.

At first some students seemed sceptical, or confused. We heard: "We've never done anything like this before," and "What should we write about?" "Nothing's in my mind," was a common complaint. "Then write about *that*," we said. "What does 'nothing' mean to you?"

As the weeks progressed, participants came to relish class time – the hours during which they could release their day to the blank space of the page. Students filled pages with thoughts about childhood memories, the future as well as their triumphs and losses – from a cell phone to a homeland.

One of the many benefits of free writing is that there is no time for censorship, for the inner critic to chime in and say, "What is this?" or "Where is this going?" Generating freshly-minted words was the goal of every session, empowering students to keep the pen moving, to reach for the next word, and to write through those nagging thoughts that so often stifle creative energy and stop the flow of words.

Free writing allows writers to sink deep into themselves and let images, scenes, and thoughts bubble up free of self-censorship. In *Writing With Power*, Peter Elbow, an emeritus professor of English at the University of Massachusetts at Amherst, says, "When people first do free writing they usually experience an immediate release from pressure. It doesn't matter what words come out. In the absence of danger, they find new words, thoughts, feelings and voices they didn't know they had. Most of all they discover that the process of writing doesn't have to be an ordeal."

After the initial writing exercise – in which everyone participated, including the two of us – we went around the table and read what we had written. This form of active engagement and sharing was a new experience to these students; it created a vulnerable but safe haven within which to share all material created during the workshop series.

We then took turns reading aloud pre-selected examples of strong writing across a range of genres and themes, including persuasive personal essays from a variety of sources: Arabic essay collections, articles from *The New York Times*, and various magazines, including *Muslim Girl*. We also read poetry by Rumi and other poets, and excerpts from memoirs. After the day's chosen selection, the group would discuss its subject matter, as well as the style, voice, tone, and point of view in each piece of writing. Then, as a large group, we brainstormed aloud ideas the writing sparked, prior to practising specific writing techniques, such as writing in the present tense, or from different points of view.

By the end of the workshop series, we saw a marked change in the participants. They were more deeply engaged in their writing and more comfortable expressing their opinions and ideas on the page. They wanted more still, so Carol has made several trips back to Qatar to write with these and other students.

The Books: Qatar Narratives; Qatar: Then and Now

To date we have published two essay collections, *Qatar Narratives* and *Qatar: Then and Now*. Those volumes featured expatriate writers from other countries in the Middle East, Americans, and several Qatari nationals.

This volume is devoted exclusively to the essays by Qatari nationals that first appeared in the earlier books. Some of the narratives have been edited by the writers; they saw ways to improve and update their original work, as a few years have passed since the first publication. The reworked essays reflect the writers' more precise word choices as well as their growing maturity of style. The updated profiles of the contributors also demonstrate that they have transitioned from one stage into another in their lives – from university student to young professional, from professional to graduate student, etc. The revisions reflect these important developments, which are significant in the life of any writer.

What remains the same in this new volume is the diversity of themes from the first two books; the essays range in style from the very personal to the global: narratives of childhood memory, essays about future aspirations, and differing perspectives on current issues. Our desire has been to provide space for a range of voices to express the full complexity and richness of life in Qatar. Many of the writers are part of the 'hinge generation', those living the transition between tradition and modernity. They are acutely aware of the challenges inherent in juggling the competing demands of familial, cultural, and professional obligations.

Since the original publication of these essay collections in 2008 and 2009, writers from the series have gone on to explore other avenues of literary expression and publication. One contributor to *Qatar: Then and Now* co-edited the third volume in the series, *Dreesha: Lamahat Men Qatar* or *Glimpses of Qatar*. Others have enrolled in writing workshops, pursued graduate study, and made writing a central part of their lives.

Support for this series has come from the Waqif Art Center and the Center's fund called 'Finding Your Voice.' Other sponsors include Al Waab City, HSBC Bank, the American Embassy, and Qatar University. With gratitude for all that support, and ideas for future publications, it is our pleasure to present these writers to a wider audience once again, hoping as before to convey an ever-deepening sense of the complexity of life in Qatar.

The reader may note spelling variations amongst the essays in this volume (which reflect the multinational educational background of the contributors). In most instances we have retained the original US or British spellings of the writers' original texts.

Carol Henderson and Mohanalakshmi Rajakumar
April 2010

A Different Life Now

MARYAM AHMAD AL SUBAIEY, an aspiring writer, graduated with a degree in Political Science from the UK and is working toward her Master's in Development Studies. Maryam works as a political researcher during the day, but at night she turns to her true passion, which is writing. She has been an active member of the literary society, contributed numerous essays, articles in Woman Today magazine, and is a popular blogger. She has participated in many writing programs and presented her own workshops in both Arabic and English. Inspired by the first two volumes of the Qatar Narratives series, Maryam generated the idea behind the third volume of the series, a photo-essay book Dreesha that she co-edited. Currently she works as an intern in a publishing house in London. She is working on her first book and aspires to be a well-known published author.

THEY ALL SAY LIFE is different now. Yes, it is different, much more modern, much more tolerant, and much better for women. I always imagine: What if I had been born in a different era? Would I have been given the opportunity to study abroad? Would I have been able to work and improve my talents? Sometimes I even think of the small things, like meeting my friends in a café and going out with them on trips. Or even going to the beauty salon to have my hair done or to the spa for a massage. If I had been born, as a girl, in the Gulf, more than fifty or seventy years ago, would I have been able to enjoy these simple things? Things I believe are not only privileges but also rights. I will never know for sure. Because sometimes I think that, despite the changes, my life, in certain aspects, is not that different from my grandmothers'.

I have two grandmothers whom I love so much; I visit them every week and I like listening to their stories. Even though they are from the same generation, have typical old names and both wear the *batoola* mask, they are extremely different. My grandmother from my father's side is originally from the Emirates. Her mother taught her how to read and write. She has a petite figure and is very calm, very modern. She likes things to be neat and tidy; she doesn't like a lot of noise or being around too many people. She only speaks wise words and never leaves the house, unless for something very important. She spends time in the *hotta*, the barn, at the side of the big house, checking on the goats and chickens. Then, she goes to the kitchen to check on the cook. After that she checks on the flowers in her garden. She always carries a small key in her pocket; it's the key to the storage room. No maid can fool her and steal an extra can of milk or take a few more eggs, or claim that the plates and pots were already broken! She knows everything and manages everything.

One day she was telling me how the house was different long ago. There was a dining room in the other *majlis* but, because no one liked to eat on the table, they just removed it. Then she pointed at the small *majlis* and said, "Your uncles and grandfather used to eat here."

"Where did you use to eat?" I asked.

"In the same place."

"You didn't eat together?" I asked.

"When they finished," she said, "your aunties and I would come and eat."

"Why didn't you bring your plates and eat together?"

"We used to eat from their big plate after they finished," she said.

My face expressed a big exclamation mark and I said, "What?"

Surprised, I paused for a bit then asked, "You mean that you used to eat what was left on the big plate?" and she said, in a calm pleasant way, as she always does, "Yes."

Trying to understand what I had been told, I asked, "Was it fine with you to eat leftovers?"

"Oh yes," she said. "It was a long time ago. It was common."

I couldn't help but ask, "What if you were hungry and they finished all the food?"

My grandmother laughed and said, "If it's finished, it's finished!"

I was quiet for a while, looking at her, again trying to

understand what she had told me. She didn't seem mad about it; it seemed normal to her! That was the tradition. I immediately imagined myself in that situation. I would have probably had a nervous breakdown!

My other grandmother, on the other hand, is a pure *bedwen*; she told me that she used to live in a tent, which she helped make herself. She also used to bring the water from the well. She is a loud, cheerful person who loves to go to the desert, even in the summer. Somehow, for her, the weather is always lovely there, even during the burning summer heat.

She would say, "What wonderful weather; it brings your soul back." She is kind of chubby and never stops moving. She shows affection, sometimes too much, and always likes to give things away.

One time I asked her, "Why do you go to the desert in the heat? It's unreasonable."

"I have nothing left but those goats and chickens there," she said. "They keep me occupied, and what else am I going to do? Plus, it reminds me of the old days."

My mother's mom is illiterate, stubborn, and has a weird hobby of building and demolishing. The back of the house used to have a room for the maid and a kitchen. Now you can see the back of the house at the front of the house; there are two new kitchens, a storage room and something else that I never figured out the purpose of! The same thing happens at her camp in the desert, building and demolishing, until you can't tell the kitchen from the toilet from the storage room. But, what I find incredible about her is her rare talent for memorizing difficult *bedwen* poetry – after hearing it only once. She is an encyclopedia for old *bedwen* poetry, and she enjoys telling us her poetry with passion as much as she enjoys watching *bedwen* soap operas.

This grandmother has truly suffered in her life. She was an orphan and was raised by her aunt. She was considered a burden and was rushed forcefully into marrying a man who was as old as her father. She was nine years old.

"I was playing with the kids," she told me, "when my aunt called me and changed my clothes and told me to wear *batoola* because I was a woman now. Then she gave me a piece of candy and handed me over to my husband. I couldn't live with him. So he divorced me and they married me again to another man who was even older than the first one. I had a son from him, and I was divorced again. Then I married your grandfather and had your mom and uncles and aunties."

Both of my grandmothers amaze me with their patience. I wonder if I could ever handle the same injustices they have suffered. But today's situations are at a different level. I remember one time when my younger brother asked me where I was going. I thought to kid around with him and said, sticking my tongue out, "None of your business."

He laughed because he saw that I was kidding, but my mom heard me and started shouting, "THIS IS YOUR BROTHER. HE IS A MAN AND HE IS RESPONSIBLE FOR YOU. DON'T DISRESPECT HIM LIKE THAT. YOU'D BETTER TELL HIM WHERE YOU ARE GOING."

I was surprised at my mother's reaction. I immediately said, "Does it make sense that I, being the oldest, ask permission to go out from my younger brother? I don't see him telling me where he goes so why should I?"

Then she added, breathing loudly, "You girls are such a

burden! When are you going to get married so I can get rid of you?"

I never understood why girls were considered a burden and were always rushed into marrying young. I believe that the current generation should not pass those gender discrimination ideas to their children. Yes, men and women are different, but neither should suffer injustice because of gender. I, at least, would love to teach my children that they are equal; I will teach my son that he won't be punished less than his sister because he is a man. Whatever mistakes they make, they will be equally punished, and for whatever good things they do, they will be equally rewarded.

My life is so different from my grandmothers' with much more freedom, with many more rights, but always with a fight! Somehow life is still the same when it comes to certain aspects. We are, after all, women.

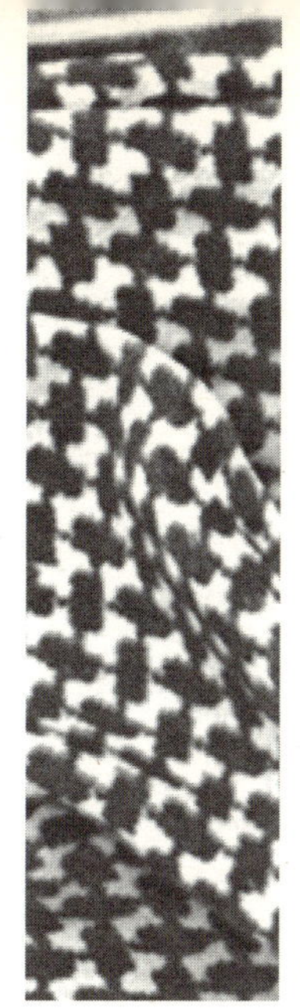

Coming to Doha

Mohammed Jabor Al Kubaisi was born in Doha and spent his childhood in Al Shamal, a small town where his tribe lives about ninety-five kilometres north of Doha. He is a student at Texas A&M University, majoring in Petroleum Engineering. He hopes someday to use his engineering skills to create a permanent footprint in the development of his country, in order to show that people living outside of the city centre also have contributions to make.

Everyone loved this small, quaint town, and every guest from across the seas was amazed by its people who had lived here for centuries. It was a calm and peaceful land where you could hear the murmur of the sea and birds singing. The air was clean and full of happiness. Even when you were sick, this land would bring life to your body, cleansing all your organs. People were kind and generous. Although they were poor, and did not have enough food for their daily meals, they offered any guest who visited them hospitality that he would never forget.

What is this land I am talking about? Who are these people? It is Al Shamal, the original home of most tribes of Qatar, including my tribe, the Al Kubaisi. This town, about ninety-five kilometres north of Doha, was also home to many other tribes: Al Mannai, Al Naimi, Al Kuwari, Al Kaabi, and Al Mohunadi. These tribes were like one hand; they worked together, fished together, and, most importantly, they were friends in war.

Now all my tribe members in Doha have left their original home, leaving behind all those good memories, the beauty of that hard-working time, the fantastic mud houses they had built, and the old stories related to the sea. All these memories were left behind the doors of their old houses. They were unhappy but it was time to move to Doha.

You see, Shaikh Khalifa Bin Hamad Al Thani, our ruler in that era, approved an order for all tribes in Al Shamal town to come to Doha. The first tribe that agreed was ours. Most of our family (the tribe) moved to Doha, including my uncles. They did not move directly after the order; some of them stayed there and some came looking for jobs in Doha.

The men, including my uncles, applied for jobs with Qatar Petroleum Company and to live in Doha. When they were accepted, they did not come to Doha directly. They had two houses, one in Al Shamal and one in Doha. The one in Doha was for men who worked in the city and the one in Al Shamal was for the women and their children. It was hard for their children to be educated away from their parents and it was hard for my uncles to drive back and forth from Doha to Al Shamal.

Shaikh Khalifa Bin Hamad listened to this story and he realized that this was a difficult situation. The children's schools were only in Al Shamal. So he built a neighbourhood in Madinat Khalifa that was totally new, just for the Al Kubaisi family, with new houses and new schools. The neighbourhood was not near Qatar Petroleum Company, but it was still in Doha, which meant it was much better. Eventually, the entire tribe moved to Doha.

The tribe members, including my father and grandfather, tried to adapt to the new situation. In Madinat Khalifa there was no sea for fishing, no birds singing, and no huge boats for diving to look for pearls. However, the thing that made the new situation easy to accept was that we were also together, home by home, side by side, and wall by wall, living again in one family without distances straining our close family bonds.

My family began to adapt to the new situation. Children now became educated by modern learning in schools. Some of them have completed their studies abroad in countries like the United Kingdom and the United States. In addition, houses are now provided with electricity and air conditioners, unlike the mud houses that were not connected to electricity. Of course my father and grandfather did not particularly like this new situation, but it was a stage of adaptation and they were satisfied with their destiny.

Now it has been years since the early adaptation stage. A new generation has come, born in Doha. This generation is well-educated and has the ability to work and learn more about life. Although they were not born in Al Shamal and they do not know how hard life was in that time, they have heard many stories from their grandfathers, amazing stories that show the value of creating one family, of facing dangers, and of travelling across the seas to provide daily meals.

They left their home but they did not forget their history. They came to Doha and they brought with them a rich history of sacrifice. My grandfather, known as Essa Bin Khalifa Al Kubaisi, Shaikh of Al Kubaisi at that time, wrote a poem after he had visited Al Shamal again:

We came to you our land
We will not fear the darkest nights
We came to you our land
We will not hide the shining sun.

We will not forget our original land, we will not forget our history, and we will live to teach the new generation the meaning of creating one family and sacrificing in order to live a satisfied life.

At the same time, my parents and all the family members were very happy, even though they tried to forget the sad moments of leaving their home and how really hard and painful they were. Every woman sang a beautiful song to her children; every man took his sons and left them in the *majlis* to learn more about poetry; every old man and woman walked with their narrow sticks and met young children in the halls with a lovely smile that could carry the bright future to them.

Years and years after leaving Al Shamal, the sad moments are now gone. The life that was in Al Shamal is now in Madinat Khalifa, opening the *majlis* of every house for any guest, arranging the sword dancing (*Al-Ardah*) for every Eid. The tribe leaders were really delighted and over the moon. Seeing the family members bonded together again was just like a dream. They expressed their happiness by taking the rifles from their houses and shooting into the sky with much laughter. I said from my heart, "Thank God we are one family again."

In the end, "No history, no present" is a traditional saying of our grandfathers that indicates the importance of family history. Remembering these events from the past helps us to live with comfort and happiness because we will carry this message to the coming generations. We will tell the new generation how we were and how we are right now, making sure to pass on our meaningful history.

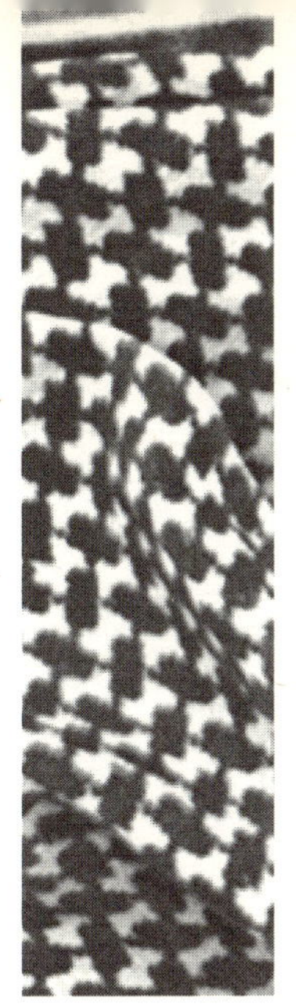

The Secret Smile of Change

MASHAAEL SALMAN RASHID is a graduate of Qatar University who majored in Computer Engineering. As a student Mashaael was an active participant in campus life and a member of the first University service learning trip to the West African country of Mauritania. In Mauritania she learned what a fortunate life citizens and residents of Qatar have and the importance of grass roots organizations to their communities. She works at Qatar Central Bank in its IT department.

THE CAR SUDDENLY STOPPED.

Here we go; everything is finished, no need to think about my dreams, just forget them! I thought.

At this moment my future was to be decided. Would my brother turn the car around and go home or would he carry on to the college?

Why hadn't I handled this in a different way, why hadn't I told them before?

I held my breath. My brother looked at me and I waited for his decision.

Oh, my God. How had I gotten myself into this situation?

To start from the beginning, we have to go back a week.

Studying at university for me was a dream that took a long time to realize. I finished high school with excellent grades, which helped me get a scholarship to study in the Academic Bridge Program. As the name suggests, this program was designed to help students make the transition between studying at high school and university: it was a bridge between the two. The ABP would teach students who had just finished high school the skills required to study at university: for example, English, maths, computing and communication skills.

I was so happy when I got a scholarship that I hadn't expected; I felt excited. It would be a new experience after finishing high school, and I would be able to get a good education. Unfortunately, one day I got a phone call that threatened to destroy my dreams before they'd even started. I was watching TV happily with my sister when suddenly my phone rang with an unknown number.

When I answered, a lady was asking about me. A lady I didn't know. This wasn't a real surprise, not as much as what she told me next.

"We want to inform you that the Academic Bridge Program classes are for both boys and girls," she said, "and we need to be sure that you will agree to study in our program under these conditions."

I was shocked. I remained silent for several seconds, and thought to myself: Excuse me, what are you talking about? It can't be!

We didn't really have mixed-gender study environments in Qatar. All our public schools are separated: girls' schools and boys' schools. I said to myself: all of my dreams are gone with this new system! It was a difficult issue to deal with. If it were only about me, then I think I would have accepted it, but what about my family? I thought that it was impossible for my family to let me enrol in a *mixed* educational program. If there had been a previous experience like this for someone in my family it would have been easier to convince them, but unfortunately there wasn't. It would be the first time to put into practice a mixed educational environment in Qatar. All of these thoughts came to my mind while the lady was waiting for my answer. In fact, I didn't have an answer to tell her. But she needed to have an answer and she needed it straight away. If I said "No" then all my dreams were finished, and if I said "Yes" what about my family?

The silence was becoming embarrassing and then suddenly I heard myself saying, "Yes, no problem. I will be happy to be one of the first students to try this new experience!"

As I pronounced these words, I felt as if there were someone else talking. I had to defend my dream, although I wasn't sure how.

I couldn't tell my family about it, at least not now: I myself hadn't gotten used to the idea. How to tell them, how to convince them? I had no idea! My life would change a few days later: an interview was required to specify my English level. My brother was giving me a lift to the Academic Bridge Program building to have the interview. He didn't know yet about the new system.

Actually, I thought, if I didn't tell him and he discovered later, when we arrived, it would be worse. I was so afraid that he would turn the car around and go home if I told him but I was left with no choice. As we were approaching the Academic Bridge Program campus, I started to talk to my brother.

"This program is really a great opportunity for Qatari students to improve their skills and to be able to learn how to survive at university."

He couldn't guess why I was telling him this. He thought I was happy and nothing was wrong.

"Actually, there is a small problem," I said, "and I really wish you could understand and help to solve it."

"What are you talking about?" he asked. By the time I finished telling him there would be boys and girls studying in the same place, the car suddenly stopped.

I thought: Here we go, everything is finished. No need to think more about my dreams, just forget them. He was surprised that I hadn't told my family before, and that I was just making this decision by myself, which was not true. I wanted to show him the place first and talk to people there, so he and I would know what it was like.

He looked at me, and I waited for his decision. I was overcome with relief as he started the car again and drove until we arrived at the building. In fact, I was lucky, because the place was almost empty; there was hardly anyone there, and it seemed quiet. There were not many boys around, which was really good at that moment.

I had an interview to determine my English level and it went well. But that didn't matter; it was what happened later that mattered. Unbelievably, I convinced my brother and my family to let me enrol in the Academic Bridge Program.

The following week, for the first day of class, I was really nervous, scared, excited and happy. When I arrived I was shocked, because unlike on the previous visit, now there were many students.

Where am I? I thought.

I was seeing so many boys.

Oh my God, how will I be able to come every day for eight hours and stay with these boys in the same building? How will I be able to study with boys in the same classroom? I was asking myself this as I walked through the building.

I was nervous. I couldn't look left or right. I just walked straight, pretending no one was there. I couldn't say "Hi" to any of my friends because I felt too shy to talk. I felt all of our conversations would be heard by the boys, so I just kept walking until I arrived at the meeting room. It was a big room.

Unfortunately, I arrived late with some of my friends. We couldn't find seats in the rows at the back, where the girls were sitting behind the boys. The only empty seats were in the front row. So that was where we sat, with all the boys' eyes on us as we took our seats.

I wished a hole in the ground would open up and swallow me at that moment.

Congratulations, Mashaael, that's what happens when you're late on the first day, I told myself. What a bad start!

The director gave a speech for the opening day of the Academic Bridge Program. He said it was a great opportunity for the students to be enrolled in a program that would help them to gain the required skills for studying at university.

I hope I can focus on what I will learn now, I said to myself.

But that was easier said than done: the first class at the Academic Bridge Program was bad.

I was still nervous. I couldn't behave naturally. Usually, I would feel free to talk, to get used to any new place quickly. But this time the situation was different. For the first time in my life I was sitting in the same room as boys. I could hardly talk or think. I was mostly just listening.

They arranged us in the class so that the boys were on one side and the girls on the other. We were in the same class, but without sharing any conversations.

"Good morning. Each one of you should now introduce him/herself to the others," the teacher said. I was really embarrassed, I felt too shy to talk. What would I say? I thought. How would I talk?

I will never forget my first presentation: it was terrible!

I was standing in front of all the students. My face turned red from embarrassment. My voice shook while I was talking; I had prepared to talk for ten minutes, but I only spoke for three. When I had practiced the day before, I really did well. Unfortunately, I couldn't do the same for the real thing. Because in the real thing there were boys present and in my room at home I had been alone. I forgot everything and was only focused on finishing the presentation. After the presentation, my teacher, who usually let the other students ask if they had any questions, asked me to have a seat immediately. This was kind of her. She could see that I was hardly standing.

But then, as time went by, I got a chance to do another presentation. I made up my mind that this one would be totally different from the last. I would know exactly what to say within the required time, and not sit down before. My topic was about seatbelts.

I thought: how can I make this presentation interesting?

I had an idea, which was to have an interview with one of the students who drove. At that time, none of the girls had a driving licence.

There were four girls and six boys in that class. I thought: who should I choose to interview during my presentation? It had to be a boy. Actually, there was one student all the girls could talk to. He was fat, friendly, and easygoing.

But still, I had to think how I could choose him in front of all the others; I needed a good reason. So I made a plan. I'd write the names on small pieces of paper and pick one paper randomly, which would be the one I'd interview. I had to make sure to pick the fat boy whom I'd feel comfortable interviewing.

There was only one way to be sure to pick his name, which was writing his name on all the slips! During the presentation, I told the students that I didn't know who I should choose to interview, so to be fair I'd choose randomly.

I smiled a secret smile but no one could guess why.

Yeah, it is fair, I said to myself.

To make it seem more plausible I let one of the boys pick the paper from among the others. I pretended I was surprised when he chose the name of the fat boy.

I was really good at controlling myself, making sure not to laugh.

I am convinced he believed one hundred percent that the draw wasn't planned. Thank God they didn't open the other papers!

Sometimes we feel that there are impossible things that we will never be able to do. We give up before we really try. The Academic Bridge Program was the first step I took towards my future.

I was a shy little girl who didn't know how to deal with different types of people. I was limited in my closed, old-fashioned school environment. I couldn't feel the change in me during the year of studying in the Academic Bridge Program.

It was later that I could feel it: I could see how much my character had improved. All my fears had gone; I felt different. I could deal with all students, girls and boys. I learned not to judge before getting involved and seeing things clearly. I learned to think beyond the borders and to see things from a distance. And it wasn't just for me; for our country, Qatar, too, it was a big step. My conservative society took a bold step and, from what I can see, it has succeeded.

A lot of people were afraid of these changes at that time and some still are. They thought it was too much, it should happen more slowly; change should be more gradual.

This idea is normal. Sudden change is worrisome: we get used to things being done in a certain way. But that's not a reason to turn our backs on change.

Yes, there will be some problems and some mistakes. But that's inevitable; that's how life is.

What I am sure of is this: if you want to make progress you have to take a risk. You can't separate the two. Even if it's taking a new route to get to work there's a risk. You might get lost and be late to the office. But it might give you a new way that's quicker and that's a more comfortable ride to work every day in the future.

Let's stay confident and forge ahead.

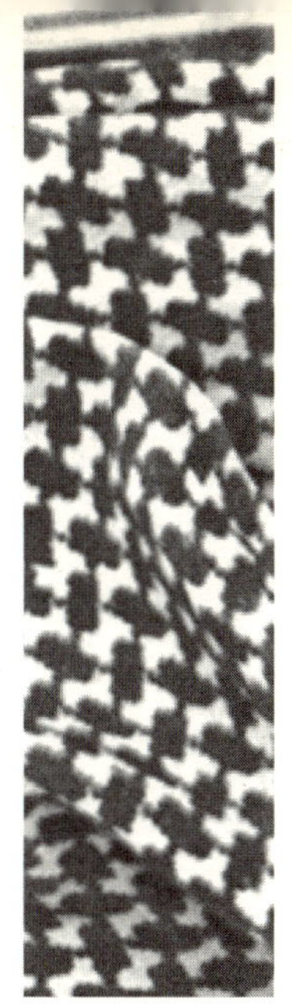

The Sidra Tree

SAAD RASHID AL MATWI is a student at Carnegie Mellon University in Qatar, majoring in Business Administration with a minor in History. He has been attracted to the world of history and literature since childhood. He believes that Qataris as a society have the ability to preserve traditions, culture, and values, while developing and modernizing the country. He was the Arabic translator for a section of the fourth book in the Qatar Narratives series, Hazawi.

IT IS A THURSDAY AFTERNOON. The weather is pleasant; the northern wind is cool while the sun is shining with warmth. Spring has always been my favourite season; it reminds me of the days when I used to play with sand in our backyard in our old house in Al Sadd. My grandmother used to say that our old house was one of the first houses to be built in the Al Sadd area. My family moved there in the early 1960s and we lived there until a few years ago. This house was renovated and expanded several times. Since the time we left this house, I haven't come back until now.

Today I go back to the old house to meet one of my childhood friends. As he is late, I walk into my old house that is empty now. I always played in the sand here and tried to build a small house or a castle. I walk around to the backyard. Over there is the sheepfold where my grandmother used to keep her sheep; one of my daily duties was to take care of them. The fold is empty now. I walk toward the kitchen slowly, the voice of my grandmother still in my mind and calling me loudly.

"SAAD ... SAAD come to me now."

The kitchen door is closed, yet I still remember the trick for opening it. It works this time too. Our kitchen, also empty, was my grandmother's own territory; no one was allowed to do anything, or to move anything without her permission. She knew every spot in her space well, knew how to manoeuvre; she knew the place of each tool and item. Our kitchen was typical, with two ovens, two fridges, and shelves for spices, sugar, salt, etc. The special thing about our kitchen was that it had three doors that are still there. One leads to the backyard, the second to what we used to call '*al-hoosh al-shamali*' (the northern yard), which is the older section of our house. The last door leads to *'al-hoosh al-janobi'* (the southern yard). In the middle of the southern yard stood a huge sidra tree as old as our house.

Once upon a time, this tree used to be wrapped with green leaves during the spring. Today it stands naked. In the space between the three doors, my grandmother would lay her carpet made of palm fronds and sit. Like a queen sitting on her throne, she would settle on the ground, sun reflecting on her golden *batoola*, emphasizing a wide smile beneath it. She wore orange *jalabia*. I always loved this colour on her, because it made her shine like the sun. Now I can almost smell her Arabian coffee. She had a special recipe for making coffee; it had an amazing flavour. I have never since drunk Arabian coffee like hers, and never will.

I hear her voice again – calling on me – taking me to that time when she gave me orders and I obeyed.

"Saad, take these bags of bread to our neighbours. It's Thursday. Did you forget?"

I see myself taking the bags and walking in an automatic manner through the southern yard to the *majlis*. The yard now is covered with dust and the ground is covered with leaves from the sidra tree. I pass through our *majlis* toward the outer door. I enter the *majlis* and cross it to get to the outside door that takes me to the neighbourhood. I can hear my uncle's voice bragging, "This door was never closed." It is closed this time I visit. The wooden door squeaks, the carpets are worn out, and the rain has leaked and damaged the roof. The males of the family used to gather here every day, especially on Fridays. Memories start to come into my mind, memories of my uncles sitting inside entertaining guests. I hear voices of my relatives and my family's friends, approaching after performing the *al-jama'a* prayer, and I am running back and forth to the kitchen to bring the dishes for the Friday lunch.

Taking the old path I walked every Thursday, I follow my small footsteps and walk out of the door and cross the football field opposite our house. The football field was not a proper field but a space covered with sand, yet it was more than enough for us. I walk, just like I always did, to Umi Metha's house.

She was as old as my grandmother and her house is the closest to ours, with only the field separating the two. I remember how each time the ball flew over her walls and landed inside her house, she would deflate it before giving it back, and shout, "Boys ... come and take your ball."

I walk toward the ground-floor house as I used to do, but there is no house standing there, only a huge white wall. I don't remember that there was such a wall. I raise my head, and I see now a five-storey building. I walk around the building and I find a glass door. This door is facing the street not the field as the old door used to.

I turn left, as I always used to, toward Umi Shama's house. She was even older than my grandmother; she lived in this house alone with her daughter, her husband having died years earlier. When I visited them, they used to give me candies and chocolates and always asked me about my studies. I approach the house and find that the wall is destroyed and the house is under construction. There are no human beings inside. I go inside to the living room, and there are no candies and chocolates this time; there is only concrete and cement. I go back to the street looking for something or someone. And I find nothing familiar. I see people, workers from South Asia, North Africa, Europe, and all around the world.

I walk back and retreat into our old house through the *majlis* door. But the door is closed. I open it and walk towards the yard looking for my grandmother. She is not there sitting on her rug, not even standing in the kitchen. My grandmother passed away ten years ago, but I can still smell her scent in her bedroom and in the southern yard. Can a person die and leave their scent behind? Her scent brings back feelings of peace and security. I long for her. I shout, calling for her. I want to say, "*Uma,* no one is there... everything has changed."

No reply. But I can hear her voice, coming from within me, saying, "*Ya olde* (Son)... Our hearts change, thus the world changed; our country is not as it used to be."

Is she talking to me or am I imagining? My cell phone rings and brings me back to reality. Was I hallucinating?

It is Khalid, one of my childhood friends, calling. We were supposed to meet at the football field. I leave the house and there he is, standing in the same place as in the old days. He's not a small kid playing football anymore. He has changed. He is a father now. He greets me and says, "Do you remember when Umi Metha, may God rest her soul, used to deflate our balls?"

I nod yes and smile back, unable to add anything.

Touring the area like strangers, we notice that the new modern buildings clash with our old houses and often with each other. You can sense that they belong to people with different interests. Some have been built quickly to start generating revenues; others are of designs and materials that were copied or brought from somewhere around the world, but surely not from our country. I remember the old houses; they all shared similar designs and were made of local materials. They were brownish in colour and didn't stand out because people didn't care about that. Now, I see different colours from light blue to dark orange. All these colours show the competition that exists between the buildings' owners, with each trying to outshine the others.

The neighbourhood has lost its meaning of unity and homogeneity. Previously a neighbourhood was made up of the same tribe, and each house had an extended family living in it. The houses stood next to each other, and their doors were always open. It was safe, as no strangers lived among them. Today the same area is made up of buildings and houses; the residents barely know each other. The buildings have become taller, the houses bigger; but our hearts have become smaller.

Khalid and I catch up and then he tells me he has to get back to his family. He excuses himself and leaves.

I watch him walking away and the memories are enveloping me again. My old house is the last one to stand in this neighbourhood. Buildings now surround it. Outside its wall and behind its closed doors, I can still see the sidra tree standing. I always thought of the sidra as similar to my grandmother and as part of me, part of myself. It was the only thing that I wished to take with me. I still remember my grandmother saying before she died, "I will not leave my house."

I can see now why she refused to leave; she was rooted in this house like this tree. Can we be like this tree? It has extended roots into the earth, but its branches never stop reaching for the sky. Can we keep our hearts rooted to our values and our culture, and still be modern?

When we moved I couldn't take the sidra with me, but I planted its seeds in our new house. The sidra there is not as big as this one, but I'm sure it will be one day. While I'm staring at the sidra, I hear the call for *al-maghrab* prayer coming from the mosque to my old house. With a smile on my face and in my heart, I feel secure again; this is the only thing that has not changed in my neighbourhood.

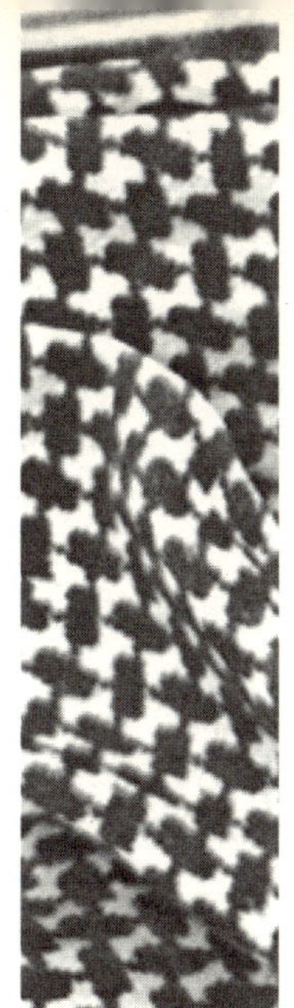

Belongingness

NOOF AL KHALIFA is a graduate of Qatar University with a degree in Finance. Although her study and work involve lots of numbers, she has always been passionate about literature.

I REMEMBER AS A KID the importance I put on the first day of school and how I got excited and nervous about what the new school year would offer me. It kind of set the tone for how the following days would be.

First days are important, but you can't depend on them because change is the constant thing in life.

I'm sitting in the car with my mother; she's busy reading some Quran. The radio is off; there's silence. We're on our way to my new school. I'm in the seventh grade and will be going to secondary school – new classes, new teachers, new friends, and I'm nervous. So, in order to delay the stress, I try to remember our recent trip to Saudi Arabia and the good times we had there. My family trip included all of us, and we all missed this critical time at school.

It's my first day in Hafusa Secondary School. I'm starting two days late. And I'm thinking that everyone is familiar with the school by now. They all know each other, except me.

I'm now standing in front of the seventh grade, in a blue classroom with a wooden door. All eyes are staring at me. I'm carrying my Hello Kitty bag, and wearing the school's ugly uniform – a beige blouse and a brown skirt; it's the first time I've worn a skirt and I hate it.

The teacher introduces me to the class. "Hello girls, please welcome your new classmate, Noof Al Khalifa."

All the girls are staring at me and I can hear them thinking: where did she come from?

"Choose a seat," the teacher says. This is a difficult decision for a thirteen-year-old kid. For me this seat will determine the rest of my days in this classroom. It feels like the weight of the world coming down on me. Where should I sit?

As I stand, wondering, a friendly girl hops up and says, "The desk next to me is empty. Why don't you sit here?"

"I'm Nadra," the girl says. She's not Qatari. It's the first thing I notice.

We became very close friends. At the end of one school day, Nadra and I were heading to the school's gate and talking.

"Noof, can I ask you something?" Nadra said.

"Sure," I replied.

"Is Al Khalifa a Bahraini family?"

"Yes," I answered.

"So why are you living in Qatar?"

"Because I'm Qatari."

"So you're not really from Al Khalifa?"

"No, silly. I'm from Al Khalifa, and I'm Qatari," I replied, in shock.

"Then why are you living in Qatar and not Bahrain?"

"Nadra, stop asking meaningless questions!" I exclaimed.

At that time I didn't have answers to these questions. But now everything is clear to me. Al Khalifa is the ruling family of Bahrain, a family with a long history.

So how can I be Qatari?

It's a long story. A story that made up a family's history, a history that many people might not know about. But we, the Al Khalifa, have always known about it and are constantly reminded of it by such questions as Nadra's.

The part of the Al Khalifa family that is living in Qatar is just like a tree that was pulled out of its original soil and planted in another. That didn't make the tree different from others. It grew up to be part of the earth it was planted in.

Because of various issues, Shaikh Abdulla bin Ahmad Al

Khalifa, who died in Oman in 1848, was not allowed to enter Bahrain. After his death, his family lived in different countries, including Kuwait, Saudi Arabia, and Qatar. The beginning of my family's settlement in Qatar was when my great-great-grandfather, Shaikh Nasser bin Mubarak bin Abdullah, married the daughter of Shaikh Jassim bin Mohammad Al Thani.

Throughout my life, I have always asked myself: where do I belong?

I know; I'm a Muslim, an Arab, and a Qatari. I come from a big family, the Al Khalifas, with complicated roots. All of this reflects on me of course, but where I belong doesn't really matter as long as I know myself.

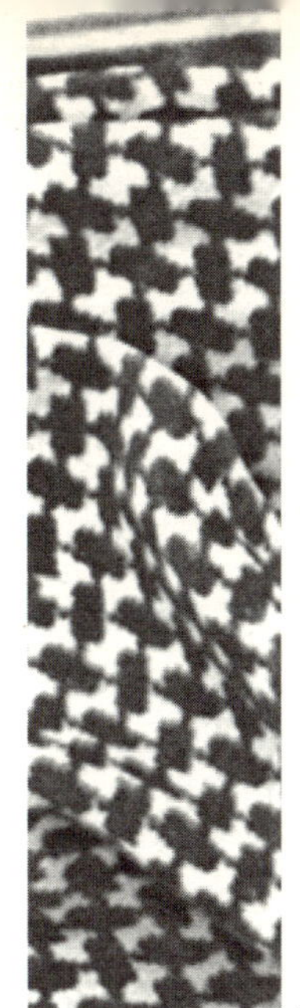

Dear Mom

Hissa Faraj Al Marri is a communications coordinator in the External Relations department at Qatar University. In the spring of 2006, she graduated from QU with a degree in Mass Communications. After her mother died, Hissa began writing in Arabic about her daily life. But during the writing workshops sponsored by this MEPI project, she started writing in English.

Dear Mom,

This is the first time I am writing you a letter since you died. It's hard to remember that you're not with me. Before you went to the peaceful life, you were my best friend; you were the only person I could talk with about the lovely stories that happened to me in school.

I liked to get your opinion on my dresses. If I felt hesitant to do something, you gave me the right decision. When I didn't do what you told me, I would discover later that you were right.

I know that it is hard to talk with you after you've died, but still I feel you with me while I'm writing my diary. So I am writing you a letter now. I lost you before my graduation day and I felt that I was all alone at that special moment.

For a long time, I kept hoping to see that you were proud of me and happy to see me graduate. As you wished, I finished my studies with high grades. I'm now working at Qatar University. I really feel that I need to celebrate my success in life. But you are not here.

I do remember when you were happy to see me finish high school and go to the university. You were supportive of me when I chose my major, but it was a very hard time, because I chose English

Literature, and I built my dreams on it, but unfortunately I didn't get the TOEFL grade for that major. I felt that destiny chose my major.

The first year in college was the worst because my cousin died and after that my two grandfathers. I knew that was hard for you, too. And now I know how you felt because it was so hard for me when you left.

I still remember your tears when your mother had pain. You were very strong. You had to face a very hard and painful time, the worst time for you.

I'm trying to be like you. I'm always trying to be strong because of you. Now I need your smile to colour my days. I need your breath to make my life beautiful.

Love,

Hissa

Note: TOEFL is the acronym for "Test of English as a Foreign Language"

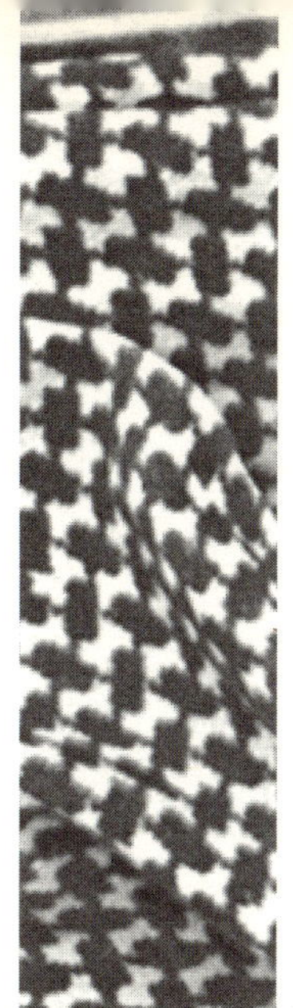

I Believe in the Spade

KHOLOUD SALEH was born in Qatar in 1988. She is Qatari, but originally from Palestine. She is a pre-medical student at Weill Cornell Medical College in Qatar. One of Kholoud's hobbies is photography; she enjoys taking pictures of different things such as landscapes and flowers. Also, she has a great interest in reading.

We believe in our past and we believe in the power that the past exerts on us. There are moments that are connected to our past that we wish had never happened. My parents had a life that was a combination of both good and bad moments. They lived in Palestine for a long time. They believed in the spade and the power of the spade. It taught them to be hard workers; it also taught them to be resilient. Their grandparents were farmers, and so my parents also worked in the fields.

Back in Palestine my parents spent most of their time with the spade; they used it at the time of planting and they used it at the time of harvest. It was the most important tool for planting. However, they were forced to leave their home country. They left behind them their beloved family, and they left behind them their lovely fields. But they were able to keep the spade values. What do I mean by the spade values? Dear readers, you'll find your answers in this text.

The life of my parents changed totally in Qatar. It was like the land of opportunities for them. They got married here. My father had a job far away from anything related to farming. He worked in Al Diwan Al Amiri, which is the Qatari symbol of sovereignty, and my mother worked as a teacher. Their values, beliefs, and hard work were transferred here to Qatar. The values of the spade were always with my parents. They tried to raise us, my brothers and sisters and me, to adopt the values of the spade. It is like an heirloom that passes from one generation to the other.

One time our professor in college asked us to bring in a family heirloom to show to our friends. Many students brought books, gold, and other things. However, I brought the pictures of the spade. The spade lies in the garden most of the time. Although it is not new, it is the most important thing in the garden. My father kept it for almost thirty-five years. I was really proud to stand up and say that this tool is our heirloom and my father still uses it. My father didn't want to disconnect himself from the past, and he also wanted to plant things with this spade. The good is planted by the past.

I always see my father working in the garden. I am amazed when I see his hard work. He never gets tired from working with the spade, even though he works in a different field. You will hold your breath when you enter our garden. The flowers lie down on the floor as if they were the queens of the garden. The leaves support their queens by making a more beautiful kingdom. The yellow flowers are jealous of the red queens so they lie over them; they are trying to hide them. The high jasmine that falls from the garage roof giggles at you with its perfume. The bees and the birds are always around, providing nice company to the beautiful garden kingdom.

This entrance will lead you to the back of the house, where the real excitement begins. My father planted there, with the help of the spade and its power, the most delicious fruits and vegetables. The red tomato can be found between the green parsley, and the high and strong lemon tree is found at the end of the garden. The yellow lemons on the tree and their green leaves make an amazing background for other fruits and vegetables. You must taste these fruits!

I can remember one of my father's friends who used to say, "You and your spade Khedr. It brings you no benefit." My father invited his friend to taste the fruit from the garden. "I know what I plant," my father said. "Gardening doesn't only bring me this tasty fruit. It also brings me joy."

My father planted the fruits and vegetables. But he also planted the spade values in us. We do what we do for joy and love. We do what we do and bring out our best when doing it, and we work hard to have the good results. When you plant the fruits, you plant them in the right place and at the right time.

My father also planted that in us: "Be in the right environment, pursue your dreams, so you can do your best in your field." The spade values didn't disappear; they were transferred here to Qatar and to us, the new generation. His words always inspired me, and that is why I want to be a very good doctor.

My siblings and I work hard to make my father proud. Most importantly we work hard and we pursue our dreams to make our country proud of us. By our hands our country will be developed; by our hearts it will be seen. Each one of us has a different specialty and a different field. We all help make the country diverse, just like the flowers, fruits, and vegetables in our garden. I'm proud to be a member of this family, the family that has learned how to value the spade.

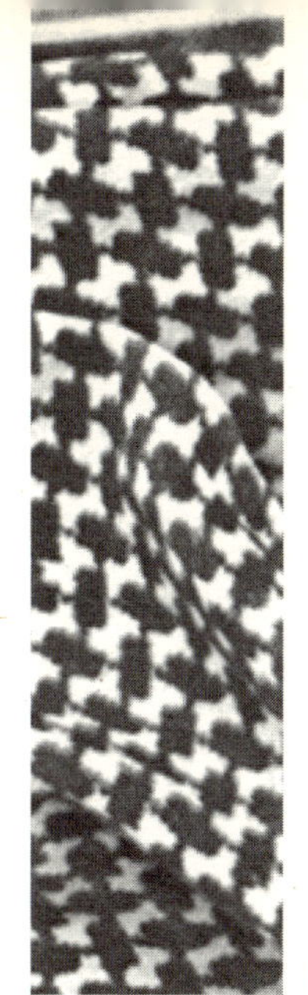

Werewolf Kiss

Noura Abdulaziz Al Suwaidi has lived her whole life in Qatar, surrounded by her large, happy family. They have travelled together often and have seen many interesting places. She graduated from Qatar University in March 2007, worked in Students Affairs as an accountant, and is now an employee of Oryx Gas. She is interested in improving her writing skills and enjoyed participating in the workshops that were part of this project.

When I'm sitting by myself wondering about my life, I sometimes ask: which part have I really enjoyed the most? I find that my childhood is the best part of my life so far. I have always loved to talk about it to everyone, and I have never gotten bored – repeating the same story a million times. For me, childhood will always be the time of pleasure, love, and imagination. I would say it is the time of honesty, but that would be only partly true. I was honest to myself but maybe not always to others.

I have two uncles who are important in my childhood stories. One is very kind. He loves to take us to the swimming pool, restaurants, and to spend lots of time with us; the other is a mystery. He looks different. He has a lone bear look and darker skin and never plays with us. Is he a werewolf, I wonder?

It's the beginning of the holy month of Ramadan. I'm an eight-year-old who loves to hang out and spend all my time in a big garden full of palms belonging to my grandfather. I spend the happiest and most beautiful childhood with my spoiled little cousin Lolo, my eldest beautiful cool sister Jojo, my slim cousin Hansam, my chatty cousin Noora, and Hamad.

Being a pudgy child makes fasting very hard for me, and also for Lolo and Jojo. One day, we grab a chicken from the refrigerator and hide it. Then we ask Grandma, "Mama, how do you cook chicken?"

"Ohhh you cute little children," Grandma replies. "You must be starving now. This is what I do. I clean the chicken with water, salt it, and directly put it in the oven."

And so that's what we do. We go to our tree house with our stolen chicken, build up a fire and start cooking for ourselves a big lunch in Ramadan. We take other things and cook them too. This would explain where all of the missing food goes during Ramadan. But no one asks us about it. We are innocent children, right?

And then there is praying. "Look," we shout, pointing. The mystery uncle is passing through the area where we're playing. He pauses for a while, opens the car window, staring at us, and says, "Have you heard the *azzan*?"

"Yah," all of us scream together.

"Did you pray?" he asks. I start worrying and wondering! What will happen if I say no? What will he do? Will he punish me?

"Yes Uncle," I blurt out finally. The words have come out unconsciously. I don't know that's what I'm going to say but I say it.

He smiles and leaves quietly, nodding in approval.

Another time we children are obsessed with buying the latest Game Boy. We decide to sell our lunches at school to make money so we can get it. We also cross the main street alone – Hamad, Lolo, Jojo and I – to reach the supermarket. This is forbidden, crossing by ourselves. We buy some stuff and sell it to the rest of the children back at Grandma's house. We are good at making money!

When the mystery uncle passes again, staring and wondering, "Hey, what are you doing?" I say, "I'm trying to collect some money to buy the latest Game Boy."

"That's very clever of you," he says. "How much more do you need?"

I smile innocently.

"You have been fasting the whole month of Ramadan," he

says, "and praying. I think you really deserve this Game Boy."

I feel happy, as though I have been kissed by a werewolf. At this point I recognize that my feelings toward my uncle's qualities and serious behavior – his weird look with a face full of hair like a long, dark black bear, his fast, direct way of walking – made me draw a picture of him exactly as the werewolf. But he isn't one!

Family gatherings, world exploring, creative expression, and initiative made me a happy child. I felt no resentment, nothing but goodwill, and mutual cooperation. I had a good upbringing, full of wonderful memories that make childhood the best part of my life.

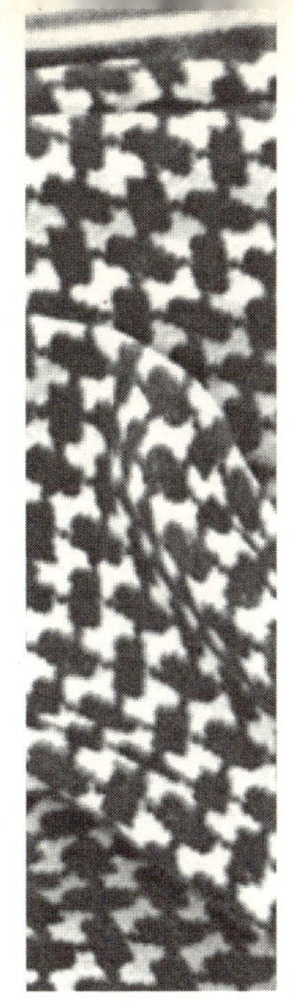

Through My Grandmother's Eyes and Mine

MOHAMMED FEHAID AL MARRI is an engineering student at Qatar University. He attended Omar bin al Khattab independent school and has travelled to the UK for English courses. He enjoyed that experience and looks forward to travelling more in the future.

I WENT TO MY GRANDMOTHER over the weekend and asked her, "Tell me about your life, Grandma. Was it comfortable or hard? What do you remember from it?"

"Come here, boy, sit next to me," she told me. "Listen, I was born in a small village called Swoda in Saudi Arabia. These villages had houses and some parks but didn't include any hospitals. It was in the middle of the desert. My own mother was very tired because the time was coming for me to come into this life. My father took my mum to *al-daua*, a woman who helped other women have children.

"My mum arrived at her house at four in the morning and I came to this life thirty minutes later, at four-thirty. When I was four years old, my mum taught me how pray, clean the house, and cook – by the time I was twelve years old I knew how to be responsible for everything. And I was married at that time. Before I got married I asked my mother, 'How old will my husband be?' She told me, 'Eighteen years old.'"

"You mean you were twelve and he was eighteen?" I asked my grandma.

"Yes, that's right," she said.

"Did you meet him before marriage, Grandma?"

"No, I didn't. After a few years, we had two beautiful girls: your mom and your aunt. My husband's work transferred him to the city. After arriving in the city, I sent your mom and your aunt to school, and from that moment I realized that everything would change."

"How?" I asked, full of curiosity.

"Your mother met her husband in a shop when she went to buy something. He saw her and he came to my husband and told him he wanted to marry her. He then went back to continue his studies in Egypt and sent your mom a lot of money from there. After some years, they finally married."

"Really!" I exclaimed.

"Yes," she said. "And they could buy so many things and you can buy so many things now. We couldn't when I was young."

"Yes," I said. "We can buy computers, phones, televisions, and radios."

"We had none of that," my grandma said. "I used to communicate with my mum by letter or see her once a week. Now you have everything you need."

She went on. "Year by year everything changed for the better in our life here. The government tries to make people's lives more comfortable and it does. The government builds a lot of facilities, like clubs, schools, airports, hotels, hospitals and shops. There is everything any person could want to be happy. And there is the university here."

"Qatar University is like any university in the world," I tell my grandma. "I am very happy since I have joined it."

"Really?" she said. "That is good."

I told her that everything I need, everything that is necessary for me to learn engineering and all the skills I need, I can get right there at the university.

"I am very happy because I don't feel lonely or freaky," I tell her. "I don't have to go to Egypt or some other place to study. I like to spend time with my friends. I don't have to be like some other students who study abroad and only get to see their families on holidays. They have to live alone, with all different people and not be in their homes with their families."

"That is good," she says. "Very good."

"I study Arabic drumming and I love to swim," I tell her.

"Yes, you swim every week or you'll be like a fish out of water," she says. "You need to swim to live."

"That is true," I say. "School is a great place. We meet different people from different places. School is the source of information and where we learn how to deal with things and other people. We have a big social world at school."

There is one last thing I want to mention and I tell it to my grandmother and to anyone else. I say it proudly, anytime, anywhere. My country is paradise for me; if I travel to another place for more than one month, I feel like a person lost in the desert without a guide, a sick person, a man without a heart.

My country is everything to me – like a girlfriend that I can never leave.

Arabian Superwoman

ROODA HASSAN AL NEAMA is a Business Management graduate from Carnegie Mellon University. She aspires to publish more works in the future, including a novel. She is working on a new business concept to introduce in the UAE as part of a young entrepreneurs initiative, and hopes to someday extend it to Qatar.

IMAGINING THE GARDEN OF OUR HOUSE, the picture would never be complete in my mind without seeing my grandmother crouching down in the middle of a bush. She was always determined to try and figure out what latest type of weed was daring to inhibit her proudest accomplishment. For me to see her in the hospital bed following her knee replacement operation was very strange. She was out of her usual framework: rushing to the market, checking on her pets, preparing lunch, setting the table, working on the garden, spending time with her grandchildren and reading the Quran before going to sleep.

Her once pleasantly plump figure was now deflated like a balloon losing its air, its essence. Her petite eyes were surrounded tightly by thin wrinkles. Her tiny button nose and her vertical slim lips seemed practically non-existent, yet still they created an overall calm balance, reflecting the kindness within. Even as she lay in the hospital bed, her tone showed concern for her responsibilities.

In a tired but serious and crushed voice, she said, "I'm worried about the house, and I'm sure nobody is looking after it like I did. Nobody is looking after your grandfather or cooking his favourite food."

Before she was sick in the hospital she would often complain about how tired she was and how nobody ever helped her, but we all knew that in her eyes nobody could meet the standards that she set. As a result, she loved to be complimented on her food, garden, pets; it was the positive feedback that gave her extra motivation and the approval of her family was always a bonus.

She was so determined to get well and be up and running, on her own two feet, before the house, as she said, "deteriorated". The care she felt for everything and everyone around her showed through her actions. She would take her time in making food for the family, perfecting the taste and the whole meal. She had a little farm in one of the corners of the house, where you could see the love and care she gave her pets. She constructed a three-area space for her goats; one area included an air conditioner for when the weather got too hot. Every day, she would make sure they were fed and felt comfortable. As her grandchildren, we would joke with her about her loving her pets more than us. She would usually reply, "Animals feel the heat too; it is the only thing keeping me away from the garden!"

Then she would laugh about a recent tantrum she'd had, screaming at one of the help for not applying her instructions to the word. "You come from jungle," she would say, steaming with anger. This was one of the few times she would actually speak the words in English. That was her nature, infuriated easily but amused easily too. She was not only active in the household, she was also active in the real estate business – building, renting and selling. Although she was not formally educated, she always pushed beyond the stereotypical grandmother capabilities.

As a young woman with five daughters, she juggled her responsibilities with her education. She was committed to learning how to read and write and finished almost six grades of school in three years. When she reminisced about that time in her life she would often impersonate my grandfather, a demanding husband who thought her time spent in night school was getting in the way of her domestic duties.

She would continue, saying, "... and those daughters! You

try and bring them up in the best way possible and provide for them. They don't have the time to help around the house *or* help me with my studies. In my day I used to wake up with the sunrise and help my mother; you know that saying is true: my heart is with my son, and my son's heart is made of stone."

Then her thoughts would lead her to remembering her mother and tears would accumulate in her eyes. Suddenly she didn't seem to be a grandmother but a child longing for her mother's arms.

Now, she is still the determined woman she has always been. She worked through her knee replacement operation, walking again but with slight difficulty. She no longer works in the garden but supervises; after all, it is her passion for life and her hobbies that keep her going. Her fad for her pets has modernized with technology; she now uses a complicated gadget to hatch chicken eggs and feed them.

My grandmother still fantasises about driving a car, saying, "If only they would allow women of my age with my poor eye sight to drive!" She complains and secretly wishes she had been younger when all this technology was around. One of our German friends described her once as "the most powerful Arabian woman I have seen".

I would simply describe her as "superwoman".

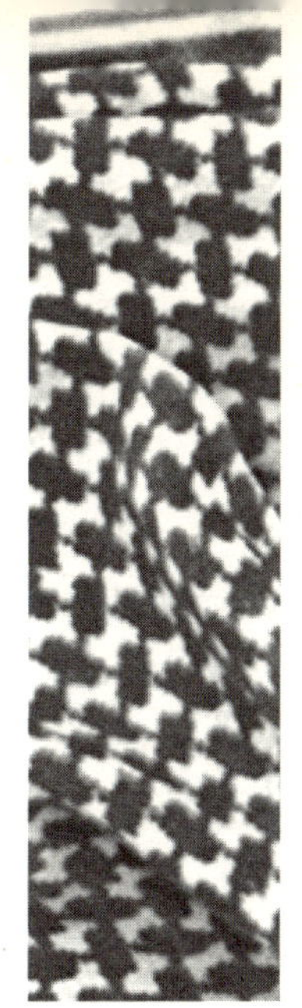

The Cycle of Life

SHAIKHA DAOUD AL SHOKRI studies at Weill Cornell Medical College in Qatar. In 2006, she received an award in Bahrain for being the best performing Qatari high school student. She attended Rabaa Al Adawia School. On Education Excellence Day in November 2007, she received a gold medal for academic achievement.

One summer evening, she was perspiring and breathing hard, holding her mother's hand tightly, weeping and agonizing. Her husband paced in the back yard. She felt she was near death and couldn't take any more pain. Then, an old woman who had a lot of experience arrived. Moving around quickly, she asked for boiling water and towels. The pregnant woman seemed to have lost consciousness, but she was still wailing. She needed help beyond that of an old woman. Yet nobody around her could do anything except ask God to have mercy on her.

A few minutes later, her moans mixed with her baby's crying. The towels, blankets and bed sheets were covered with blood. That distressing scene was forgotten when the baby was passed from hand to hand. The anxious husband stepped in and his lips curved into a smile when he heard his baby's cry. The next day, cooked fenugreek and honey were provided to the tired mother. Neighbours cleaned the home and visited her regularly. Their life was synergistic; everyone wanted to help.

The beautiful baby grew up quickly. Every day he woke up early to have breakfast with his big family – his grandfather, father, uncles, and cousins. Then he played with his cousins and friends in the street near their houses.

The most popular game was '*Spait Hai Lu Mayet*' which means 'Spait, (a male name), are you dead or still alive?' They chose one of them to act as Spait and buried his face after covering it with a *ghutra*, or scarf. Then they started asking him if he was still alive, and every time he had to respond. If there was no response, they would take his head out of the hole quickly. The winner was the one who stayed in the game the longest time.

They played many other games too, like Hide and Seek.

At the age of six, while he was playing around his house, his mother stood behind the window calling him to come in. When he entered the house, she hugged him and dried his sweaty forehead. She told him quietly that he had become a man and had to join the village Quran group, in order to start memorizing verses.

The next day was exciting; the Quran class was full of energetic children. The *mutawa'*, Quran teacher, read from the Holy Quran loudly and then all the students repeated after him, even more loudly. They started with the alphabet. That's how he learned to spell the first Arabic letter, *alef*. When he returned home, he told his relatives about what he had just learned. He was motivated to learn more in the coming classes.

A year later, the entire class and their teacher walked around the village, reciting the Holy Quran, finishing *dua'a*. People who met that parade gave them money or small gifts from their shops. Some just smiled. Of course, the happiest people were his family. They were proud of him because he had become a literate person.

After a tiring day, some years later, he found his parents waiting for him when he returned to the house. His father asked him to sit close to him and started, "Dear son, we need a happy event to visit us." His mother interrupted. "Your cousin has become a pretty lady, and we looked carefully before we chose her."

Suddenly, he couldn't say a word; he only gave a shy smile, as if to say that he understood what they wanted to tell him.

A week later, everyone was busy in the village preparing

for the big wedding. Men bought attractive decorations and butchered sheep and cows. Women prepared tasty foods such as *machboos*, a kind of rice dish served at festive occasions. Its delicious spicy smell, yellowish colour, fried nuts, and currants, mixed with mouth-watering meat, make it the main dish at weddings.

They also made *harees*, another favourite meal of the region. It consists of pounded wheat with lamb or chicken and is covered with a fresh *ghee* layer.

In another corner, ladies prepared the bride. A detailed henna design covered her hands and feet. She wore a colourful dress and her straight black hair was mixed with golden chains that dropped from a jewel crowning her head. The wedding was beautiful, complete with songs and tapes. It was a festive day for the entire village and the start of a new life together for the bride and groom.

Years later, he was pacing up and down in a hospital aisle, having just brought his wife in a few minutes earlier. In the delivery room, nurses and a doctor were giving her suitable medications to reduce the throes of childbirth. Controlling her blood pressure and heartbeat were the most important steps to ensure that everything went fine. The well-equipped room, with its advanced technology, made the operation easy.

He thanked God because he held his baby that day. The mother and baby received good care before and after the delivery; they had been looked after perfectly. The hospital provided them with a comfortable room for four days. Visitors were also welcomed.

Some years later, he was sitting in the living room watching a football match. In another room, his wife was coaching their daughter for her next test. In a corner in the house, one of his sons was playing a Game Boy; the other was playing an exciting video game. Their housemaid was cooking in the kitchen. Everybody was busy, mainly alone.

His children were enrolled in advanced schools that taught different languages, in addition to science and mathematics. They would have opportunities to join high-quality universities close to home – at Education City, Qatar University, Calgary College, or the College of the North Atlantic.

His nephew's wedding was totally different from his own. It was held in a big luxurious hall. A long table containing every type of food imaginable stood at the end of the hall. Service during the wedding was excellent.

The ladies' hall seemed like a colourful painting, the women and girls dressed in expensive modern gowns. The wedding hall, with famous brand-name perfumes, invited you to enter. The princess of the evening, the bride, wore a white gown and a bright tiara. She held a fragrant flower bouquet. That was some time ago, but he can still remember the glamour of the party.

Now, he can notice all the differences in his country between the past and the present. Life is better now, easier. The economy in Qatar depends on petrochemical industries and other rich resources. The recent changes in the constitution that put Qatar on the international map fill him with pride, a special kind of pride – pride in the achievement of the collective.

This is the one thing that has not changed. In the past, he was proud to belong to his immediate and extended family. Now, his family seems to have grown, expanded, to become a nation. He can see its influence on the larger family of nations, especially in its peacemaking efforts in Lebanon and in the generosity of its leaders toward the natural disaster victims in the United States. Like he himself, his country has gone through the process – of birth, of growing pains, of a learning process – to the celebration of its many new achievements.

His phone rings.

His nephew's voice sounds agitated as he stammers, "She is perspiring and breathing hard."

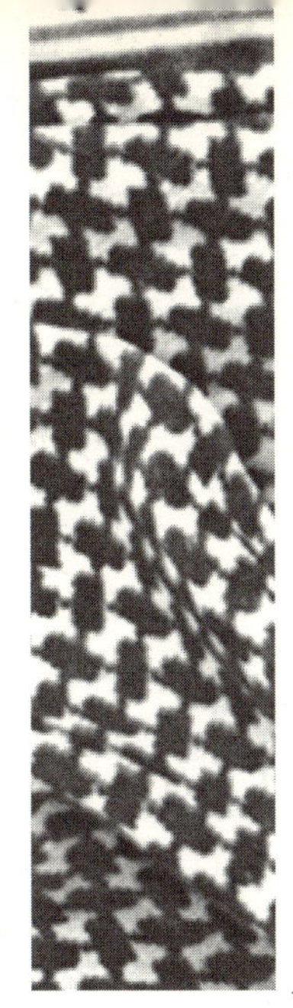

Nuptials in 1950s Arabia

Amna Abdulaziz Jassim Hamad Al Thani is a Qatari who has attended English-speaking schools since the age of five and considers English her first language. In May 2008, she graduated with honours from Carnegie Mellon University in Qatar with a Bachelor's degree in Business Administration and a minor in English. In December 2009 she graduated from The London School of Economics and Political Science with a Master's in Sociology.

TO THE SOUND OF THE *MURADAH*, a poetic dialogue complimenting the bride, my fourteen-year-old self was seated on a silk Iranian carpet and paraded by family and friends around my father's house to celebrate my wedding.

The folds of my voluminous emerald green *thob al nashel* cast shadows on the surrounding walls. The beaming *dinar*, a circular gold plate gracing my head that had moulded strips of gold sequentially chained to it, radiated dancing lights that created a kaleidoscopic effect over the emitted shadows.

I was constantly balancing myself by clutching the edges of the carpet; my hands were decorated with odorous henna in geometrical shapes, which could be glimpsed beneath the fine lattice of the intricate clinging *kufuff*, a gold hand bracelet.

This memory, related by an aged friend, provides a portrait of a traditional Arab Gulf wedding in the 1950s. Fourteen was the optimum age for a girl to be married. By then, she was expected to assume the role of a married woman, attending to household duties and bearing children.

"Getting married at such a young age is a blessing," my friend said. "As a girl flourishes in her marital home she learns her duties, priorities, and what she is expected to do to be a good housewife, therefore satisfying her husband's demands."

Unlike today, when there is increasing conflict as a result of women getting married at an older age, such strife did not occur between the couple back then, my friend explained.

"Marrying later, often with established careers, many women's priorities are already set today. Women are mainly focused on their careers, and as a consequence, they are frequently unwilling to change their priorities to suit their husband's wants."

The process of marriage started with the ritual of *milka*, held around a week prior to the wedding. The night before that, the bride-to-be would have *rashoosh* – which consisted of henna powder, saffron, and rose water, dissolved and stirred to form a thick paste – generously poured and combed through her hair. The purpose of *rashoosh* was both to fragrance her hair with a combined aroma of the ingredients and lighten the colour.

Henna would be used to embellish her hands with designs. She would spend the whole night with her hair wrapped in cloth and her hands gloved in cotton mittens, waiting for the *rashoosh* and henna to dry. The *rashoosh* and henna would be washed immediately after the *milka* was announced, and then the girl was regarded as a married woman.

"The way *milka* is handled today does not parallel the past," my friend emphasized. "It is nothing but an official, legal document signed in court authorizing marriage, whereas in the past the symbolism of 'washing the hands of henna' signified the marriage itself."

Before a girl's *milka* she used to receive the *daza*, a package of gifts combining practical household necessities with luxuries to pamper the bride. It was sent by the groom's family both to honour the bride and her parents and to demonstrate the groom's family's social status.

The *daza* contained custom-made clothes, gold, rolls of fabric, money, perfumes, kitchen utensils and dry staple food items. "The *daza* that most brides receive today are very different to what brides used to receive," my friend explained. "The *daza* changed gradually, in line with contemporary tastes and needs; a standard *daza* package today includes jewelry, money and cars."

On the evening of the wedding, the bride was prepared for the ceremony by her mother and sisters, who would dress her in her wedding gown, *thob al nashel*, a caftan-style silk dress embroidered with golden seams. It was perfumed with *dihn al oud*, an oil-based scent. Her make-up was minimal, just a fine line of *kohl* on her eyelids. Droplets of *dihn al ward*, rose oil, were sprinkled sparsely in her hair to give a pleasant infusion of rose. The final adornment was the placing of the heavy pure yellow-gold jewellery on the bride.

My friend nostalgically added, "Current brides are over made-up. They plaster the make-up on, and the wedding gowns are a hybrid of Western and modern Arabic culture. They have certainly lost the essence of simplicity found in the traditional style, where the purer look was more feminine."

Once the bride was prepared, she was seated on a carpet and carried out of her dressing room by close female relatives. Chanting the *muradah*, girls dressed in bright coloured chiffon frilled gowns, their hair groomed in tight sleek braids, lifted the bride on her carpet, to a cacophony of noise coming out of a family sitting area where anxious guests awaited the arrival of the bride. The bride's mother, her face glistening with tears of joy, led her daughter's entourage to the family sitting area. There she could be greeted by guests.

The groom on the wedding afternoon would have the *razfah*, the archaic male sword dance, performed in the *majlis*, the men's gathering area. The *razfah* usually was over at around seven in the evening. It was followed by a dinner; the groom would have his dinner with his father and other guests who participated in the *razfah*. After the dinner was over, the groom and his father would head to the bride's house.

On the groom's arrival, the bride was carried to the *khulla*, the wedding room, where she would meet her groom for the first time. My friend described what used to be considered the climax of the ceremony. "Modern couples have lost the spontaneity of their first meeting at the *khulla*," she said, "marrying after a relationship has developed between them. The tense emotions are less acute and so they don't experience the thrill that the first meeting triggered, in the past, on wedding nights."

The morning after the wedding, the bride would have her *mubaraka*; relatives and friends coming over for greetings. The bride was dressed in another *thob al nashel* which had fragments of gold, *nairat,* threaded into it. Bunches of *mashmoom*, a dainty scented flower, were intertwined in her hair, creating a cascade draping over her head. At twelve noon, the *mubaraka* would end and *ijrah*, stewed meat and rice, would be distributed to neighbours, serving as a blessing to the couple and signifying the end of the wedding ceremony.

"An Arab Gulf wedding in the 21st century typically ends with the couple travelling to their favourite destinations," my friend said, sighing. "They miss out on the little traditional customs, such as the *ijrah*. The naively innocent youthful bride has vanished, along with the little traditional pre-marriage customs we used to have, which were born out of a less complicated society. The wedding festivities today are detached from their cultural roots; it is no longer a purely

Arab experience. The old customs are seen as outdated in our developing society, but along the way, although we are losing many of the traditions, we are blending some of them into the modern style, so at least we are holding on to a small part of our heritage."

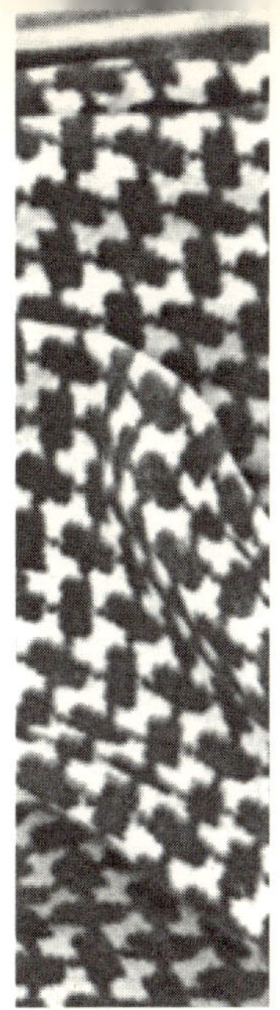

Al Kanderi: The Waterman

Buthayna Mohammed Al Madhadi is a 2010 graduate of Carnegie Mellon with a Bachelor's degree in Business Administration and an English minor. She has studied English since the age of six and has conducted research on business, scientific, social, and political topics in both Arabic and English. In 2002, she was the first prize winner in a writing competition sponsored by the post office, in which participants imagined writing a letter to a distant friend.

I'M WATCHING TV WITH MY GRANDFATHER on a Tuesday afternoon; we are watching a documentary on life in Qatar before the discovery of petroleum. The programme recaptures social life in Qatari society and the transformation that has taken place since the discovery of oil and natural gas. In one scene, they show the old neighbourhoods, old mud houses, and a man going around to the houses, carrying big buckets on his back.

My grandfather suddenly says, "You see this man. This is Al Kanderi."

"Really?" I ask, confused. "I knew a girl in preparatory school with the same family name. Are Al Kanderi on TV and the girl's family name related?"

"It is likely that the names are related," my grandfather says. And while pointing at the TV, he explains, "During that era, each area had about five *kanadrah*. They all used to carry cool, clean water and distribute it to houses. Each waterman was called Al Kanderi and all of them were referred to as *kanadrah*. This name applied to all watermen in the Arabian Gulf, especially in Kuwait. This is why a lot of Kuwaitis have Al Kandari as their last name, implying that their ancestors used to work as watermen."

Back in the 1940s, a waterman's day started as soon as the *fajir* prayer was announced. In the pre-dawn hours, he began his work. He carried two big water containers made of metal sheets in the form of rectangles, each called a *tenka*. Each of these two metal water containers hung by a rope on the end of a two-meter piece of thin but strong wood. He placed this strong piece of wood horizontally on his back, behind his neck. With all this weight on his shoulders, the man walked to the *ain*, the well, and filled his two metal water containers with water. Sometimes he stood by the shore waiting for ships carrying fresh water from other areas, like Bahrain and Basra, to fill his metal tanks. As soon as he filled his containers, the man walked towards the neighbourhoods, hoping to sell the water and make a living. This was the waterman, Al Kanderi.

Al Kanderi distributed water all day, taking short breaks every now and then from the heavy weight he was carrying. He sometimes stopped by some women sitting on a rug, cooking and selling *nakhi* and *bajillah.* He bought some and had it as breakfast on his way to the houses. Because Al Kanderi's job was tiring, he needed to stop in on shopkeepers and rest. He sat indoors with them, as their shops were sealed by palm trunks, which reduced the sun's heat. Al Kanderi and the shopkeepers would drink tea and Arabian coffee and eat dates. They would chat for a while and then Al Kanderi would continue on his way, to fill the tanks and jars in the rest of the houses with cool, clean water.

Al Kanderi was admired by children. In each neighbourhood, boys wearing *thobs* and girls in *bukhnag* played outdoors on the sand. They played *Gais*, *Al Lagfah*, and *Al Teelah.* Whenever the children saw Al Kanderi coming, they stopped playing and ran calling to him. "Al Kanderi, my mum wants you to fill our water jar" or "My mum needs you to fill our tank right away. We do not have any water." He replied with a smile, saying, "I'm coming."

Everybody knew everybody else and people kept their doors open without any fears or concerns. So when Al Kanderi reached a house, he found the door unlocked and open. Since honour and reputation issues were the women's main concern back then, Al Kanderi entered houses shouting, "Ahem ahem," so that the women in the house would be aware he was coming and cover up. At that time, it was shameful for a woman to talk to a man without covering her face. She used her *melfaa*, a black scarf that was made up of soft cotton. Some women also wore a *batoola*, a green shiny face cover, to cover the face when talking to strange men. *Batoolas* back then were worn by women regardless of their age. Now only elderly women wear them.

After the housewife directed Al Kanderi to the jar in her house, Al Kanderi walked, with his face down, looking at the floor, towards the big jar, called the *hib*. He filled it with water. Some houses also contained big water tanks that were also filled by Al Kanderi. Whenever Al Kanderi ran out of water, he returned to the closest well, or *ain*, refilled his metal water containers, and came back to distribute water to the houses.

Most of the people paid Al Kanderi on a monthly basis; a few paid him daily. People who did not fill their tanks regularly paid each time. For those who preferred to pay monthly, Al Kanderi had a special way of recording his deliveries, to keep track and make sure he got paid the right amount. Whenever he filled a *hib* or a tank with water, he drew a line on the wall of the house using a piece of coal. By the end of the month, he counted the lines to know exactly how much each family owed him. He usually got about three Robiyas per month. This amount varied from house to house because in some houses, Al Kanderi only filled *hibs*, which were small compared to tanks. Other houses, however, contained both *hibs* and tanks, which cost more.

By the mid-1960s, people had stopped relying on Al Kanderi. The government had developed ways to deliver surface water from lakes and seas into people's houses, using pipes. However, the water that reached their houses was not always purified. In addition, this new water system did not always work for everybody. Sometimes, the pipes got clogged and cleaning them required a lot of work. And because the pipes were made of low-quality steel, they rusted, resulting in polluted water. Some of the pipes leaked and broke down. Even though some people were still facing difficulties finding water at that time, Al Kanderi became less popular. By the beginning of the 1970s his job disappeared completely.

When the TV show ends, my grandfather says, "You see, dear, for Qatari citizens in Qatar, water is available for free despite the excellent water services. Kahramaa is now responsible for water treatment plants, where it sterilizes water and makes it accessible to everyone."

"It seems that Al Kanderi worked really hard," I say.

"He did," my grandfather says. "He had to because this was his only source of living. Life back then was more difficult than today. People now don't have to work as hard as our parents and grandparents did. However, back then people were like a loving and caring family. Life was simple and peaceful, and its simplicity was what gave it a special flavour."

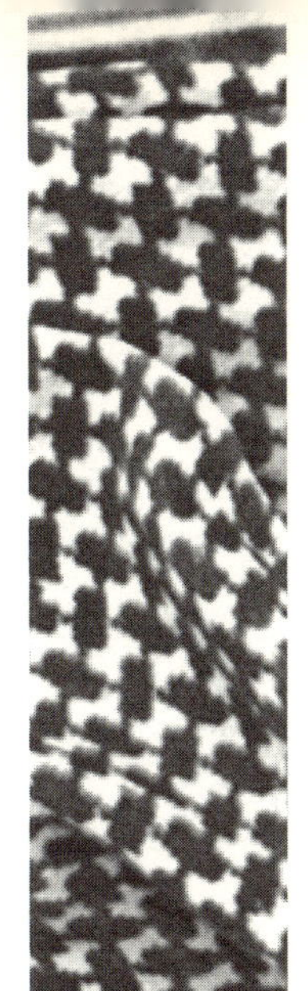

A Pearl and a Rahha

FATMA BINT NASSER K A AL DOSARI was born in a passionate rush for life after only seven months in her mother's womb and weighed 1.75 kilograms. Her early birth was only the first struggle she faced and overcame. She is a student at Qatar University, majoring in Architectural Engineering. She has a great desire for positive change in her society.

BEING A DAUGHTER OF A NATIVE QATARI FAMILY in the new millennium is easier than many may think. I know I may have a few stiff-minded elderly relatives who expect to see me wearing a *draah*, the formal gold embroidered women's clothing, whenever they see me. But I know I can claim the fate my inner self seeks.

Many girls my age feel that they were born at the wrong time and in the wrong place – a place sealed with traditions and at a time that lies in between. But I could not be happier. I have traditions that keep me secure, definite, and relieved at a time that is full of risky choices.

I was born into an environment that literally treats women as queens. For instance, when a girl is born, her baby hair is weighed, compared to an equivalent amount in gold, and this figure is given to the poor. While considering her marriage prospects, a woman doesn't have to bother herself searching for 'the one'. He will come knocking on her family's door to propose and she has the right to create her own premarital conditions, to approve or decline. Moreover, this is an environment that is rich in heritage and opportunities to develop your potential. It is a heritage with more value than the stereotypical camel-riding that comes to the minds of many when they hear the word 'Arab'. It is a heritage that is full of more potential than the gas wells, which are now also increasing in association with the mention of 'Qatar'.

Taking myself as an example of a present-day Qatari daughter, I was named – like many others – before I was born; even before my dad. My deceased great-grandmother, Fatma bint Nasser Al Ali, asked my grandfather to name my dad's (he was a baby back then) elder daughter after her. For many, it may not seem fair, but I am glad that I was named after her. Anyone who knew her, and hears her name when someone calls me, thinks of her good deeds and great reputation. She was a genuine woman who treasured everybody in her family and beyond. So, naming me after my deceased great-grandmother does not overshadow my character. It encourages me to follow her good lead as a role model and even to excel more than her by adding my own interpretation, my *samgha*, my twist. I will expand on her example by learning how to be both a *rahha* and a pearl. I will become like the refining instrument used to fulfil people's hunger. As the divers risked their lives to earn precious gems, I want to ensure my own worth.

The *rahha* was a significant tool used in daily life in our society – there was no house without one. It is the two-pieced rock tool used to sift wheat, barley, rice, and other kinds of grains. Women were usually the ones who used them as a part of their daily home chores.

I remember a story about my deceased great-grandmother and the *rahha*. She was dealing with the *rahha* just as if it was a living and sensible being; never as a rigid grinding tool. Also, I heard that she used to say that each one of us has a *rahha* inside. I realize that she meant by *rahha* our soul that God created, and our thoughts are the grains. We either sift fine grains, which lead us to a great fate and heaven or we harvest bitter grains, which lead us to a dreadful fate and hellish existence.

Our *rahhas* should be maintained and well cared for. A man or a woman should not have a vacant *rahha*; it should be constantly filled with God's love, beauty, and aims. So eventually, at that day of God's definite meeting, a man or a woman will be rewarded. I try constantly to repair my *rahba* and be a better individual – to be simple but to adhere. To look into hard and difficult aspects with the eyes of softness and easiness. To reach others and be the catalyst of change in their lives. To achieve ambitions with fewer expenses and more attempts. To be poised and energetic. To dare to dream and make mistakes. To spread unconditional humanitarian love with no preferences or judgments.

In our culture's legacy, pearls also had a great value. They were the source of living that people of the sea in Qatar depended on. Also, they were a source of pride for every woman who was fortunate enough to dangle them from her neck and ears.

I recall once when my grandmother told me a story of my late grandfather. He was in his late teens during the time before oil was discovered in Qatar. He was a well-known, continually anxious young pearl diver who travelled for months through troubled seas eagerly to locate the most valuable pearl. He felt he had made a great discovery when he spotted my grandmother for the first time and promised himself to win her love.

"When he proposed to me and our eyes met for the first time, he promised to prove his love to me in a grand way. He would prove the strength of his character and his capabilities by getting the most attractive and precious pearl ever found," she would say and sigh, each time the story began.

"He rented a shabby boat and went to a distant sea with two mates of his. It was deep water full of dangers, but his patience and willingness paid off by the two huge triumphs he won. He found two huge dazzling pearls; one he wrapped in velvet maroon cloth and presented to me as my dowry. And he traded the other in the market and gave its worth to his two fellows." She would end her story and I could see a small tear glistening in her right eye.

I always remind myself of this story and how my late grandfather risked his life to win a precious stone for a precious soul. This is how I should be. A sole identity loaded by the Qatari heritage rhythms. A bright smooth rock veiled by a consistent dark shell. A lavish jewel that a person has to work hard to gain – a unique and flawless gem – I can be both a sign of beauty and of great worth.

Anyone, girls or even guys, can be a *rahha* and a pearl. You need to accept who you are and explore yourself, apart from others' ideas for you. Traditions do not contradict with modernism; they both add value to your uniqueness and shape your identity.

Stereotypes may create mirages between your values and your heritage or your culture's potential, so you have to reveal your respect to them, educate others about them, and never feel ashamed.

Qatari women should take the opportunities that the times and the culture offer them and shine in the sweat of their hard work. There are *rahhas* and pearls in all families all around the world; they just need a little polish to shimmer and a tiny push to grow in the right direction.

Simple Life, Simple Pleasures

"There is a certain majesty in simplicity which is far above all the quaintness of wit." *Alexander Pope*

SHAIKHA YACOUB AL KUWARI is a student at Qatar University, majoring in Computer Engineering. Shaikha has been an active student at QU, representing the university as part of a delegation that attended the 2008 Zayed University Women as Global Leaders conference in Dubai, UAE. A lover of the arts, Shaikha's plans include graduate study in multimedia and design.

When we talk about the magnificence of the life we're living nowadays – the focus on higher education, the economic growth, the need to own big houses or lots of glamorous handbags or make-up or expensive cars – we often forget about what's most important: to seek peace of mind.

It always annoys me when I think about how the fast growth in technology makes us miss many simple life treasures that our grandparents enjoyed. Have you ever wondered how our grandparents managed to live without having half of what we have today, with what we wouldn't live without today? Giving this idea deep thought would bring us to a very simple realization; they lived with complete conviction that contentment is the key to happiness in life.

I read a book recently about simple pleasures. It was amazing to find that more than fifty people in the book felt happy without today's complicated daily life. Instead, they enjoyed spending their free time at home or in the company of their families. So, despite everything we have these days, due to developments in so many fields, we are still missing something – something I consider more important than most of what we have today. It is simplicity we are missing, simplicity in everything, which was the real glory our grandparents lived with.

Sometimes days pass and I don't get a chance to see my big brother or my father. It's not only because I'm under pressure to study hard or that I have exams. It's also because we're living in a big house. Each one of us has our own room and when we get extra busy we sometimes forget to ask about each other or don't have time to ask. This lack of communication has become the norm in many people's lives, not just in my family. In the past, my grandma lived in a house that consisted of only two rooms with a small yard. Children spent time together, playing in the streets. All the family slept together on the floor in one room, sharing the same blankets and telling each other about their precious daily adventures. No one lives in such houses now, though our grandparents were very happy living the way they did. Their relationships were stronger. Whenever my grandma recalls those days, she wishes that contemporary people could appreciate their modern lives the way people in past generations appreciated theirs.

Even the things that they used to worry about are different from what concerns us now. When we complicate our lives, everything gets more difficult and confusing. For instance, today's girls use fancy hairdryers to straighten their hair and to create fashionable styles. Don't you see that the number of girls suffering from hair loss is increasing? Why didn't the girls in the past suffer from such things? Elderly people who haven't used this technology have strong and healthy hair compared to young women's hair today. In the past, girls used simple techniques to take care of their hair. They put different types of oils in their hair to make it stronger and more shiny. The oil also helped reduce the curls. Even the hairstyles they wore didn't require the hairsprays or the strong hairpins that weaken the hair.

Make-up was less complicated too. Girls now wear all sorts of make-up that dries out the skin. Yet, we see that the girls today can't live without it. Many mums have skin that is much better than their daughters'. Girls now tend to use Botox to renew their skin after damaging it with a lot of techniques and toxins.

Leading a simple life didn't prevent our grandparents from enjoying their lives or from being great and successful. I believe many people think that the features and techniques required to be successful in life were founded recently, in this generation. They ignore the fact that our grandparents were also able to achieve; they were practicing those skills without planning to do so, spontaneously.

Take leadership skills, for example. These are considered some of the most important skills for success nowadays. Leadership skills have always been found in men and women; they aren't new.

Women used to have lots of these skills. Almost all of them knew how to cook, stitch, and take care of everything related to arranging the house and keeping it clean. They also knew how to raise their children with appropriate manners, even if they were living in difficult situations without their husbands, who were travelling for trading. Women were good listeners to each other and they took care of their neighbours and were always there for them in times of need. They were leaders.

Leadership isn't a new concept like many people think; it was there when our grandparents lived their simple lives. But now people think, in our rushed technology-driven lives, that leadership is something new.

I believe that happiness is something you feel in your heart not something you try to seek. Before any of us tries to search for it out there, we must look for it inside of us. Every soul that is pleased and appreciates the simple things around it, free of the continuous greediness of needing everything in life, can be happy wherever it is. To me, simply watching my mother or father smile makes me feel happy and changes my mood. When we want to be happy we can feel contentment, even in the simple pleasure of eating a bar of chocolate.

Why do I always hear lots of people say that they haven't laughed deeply from their hearts? And that they wish something would happen that would let them do so! Has life become so complicated that people have to wait for so long to laugh and to enjoy their lives? All of this makes me believe that our grandparents' simple lives were what made them feel happy and comfortable, despite the fact that their lives were difficult compared to ours.

I don't mean that we mustn't appreciate the great developments of the present time. I don't deny that these advancements have helped us a lot and thank God we're living with all of these advantages around us. But, as I said in the beginning, the hurried life we're now living makes us miss a lot of simple pleasures – and this really annoys me. In fact, I strongly agree with the spiritual writer Papa Ramadas, who believes that it's always the little things that matter most: "Simplicity is the nature of great souls."

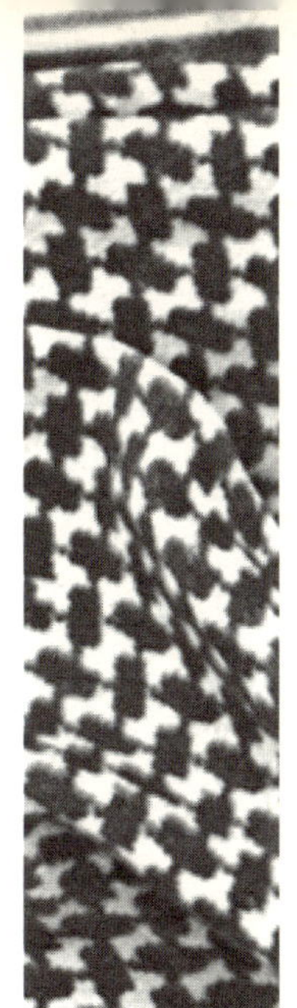

Marriage in Qatar

MOHAMMED M AL KHATER is a Qatari lawyer and graduate of Cardiff University. He has had two previous works published in the UK and plans to continue publishing in the future. He aspires to write and publish a novel one day and enjoys reading contemporary and classic fiction.

THE ACCELERATION AND PACE at which Qatar has transformed, judging just by the last decade, is staggering. So staggering indeed that the word 'rapid' doesn't seem to do it justice anymore. I think it only wise, therefore, to limit my opinion on how Qatar has changed to specific social areas in a Qatari citizen's life. I will concentrate on the social aspects that I think are in dire need of our attention.

As a result, my opinion piece may seem overly critical but I hope it's clear that I am only critical because I care about my country; I care about improving it even further and making it as great as I know it could be.

Also, I am sure the other essays in this book have touched on a lot of the positive aspects of the transformation of Qatar (one of which is the existence of this very book you are reading), but I want to concentrate on what has perhaps escaped through the cracks or is possibly a new phenomenon that got created as a side effect of the change that is ongoing here.

My main purpose is, therefore, to shed some light on these issues that need to be addressed and will be the foundations upon which we can begin to formulate a remedy for them – a remedy that can keep these social problems from spawning more complex problems that could be even harder to deal with and might end up plaguing society as a whole, prohibiting it from ever reaching its true potential.

Qatar has generally progressed at an unprecedented rate and has achieved a lot in terms of improving education, building a stronger economy, having an exceptionally high employment rate, maintaining safety, and staying true to its conservative traditional roots. Looking at these alone, one cannot help but be impressed and proud, and rightly so; these are all worthy of our pride. But dig a little bit below the surface and you will discover some deeply engrained social problems that need to be addressed. I will discuss only one of them here: marriage.

Typical marriages between Qatari families are arranged. The male's mum (usually) goes scouting for 'eligible' women and decides which one suits her son best. The son can sometimes see a picture of the 'chosen girl' beforehand (depending on the girl's family views of course – some don't even allow that). He may not speak to her, though, until after the engagement and even then, they cannot go out to a restaurant or anywhere else together unless there is a male chaperone accompanying them (usually the chosen girl's younger brother). They can talk on the phone though. So, practically speaking, they get to know each other mainly by phone and at least, in theory, if they realize they are incompatible for any reason, the engagement is off.

If the engagement fails, the male's family goes back to square one, with the mum scouting for other eligible women. This is a purely traditional phenomenon and it is absurdly outdated. I understand that this was the norm back in the days of our parents' generation, but the difference between the world that we, the new generation, live in, and the world they lived in is huge. We, the young adults in Qatar, are a testament to one of the biggest generation gaps that ever existed in this world – a generation gap that has been widened beyond belief by the unprecedented development Qatar has been through and by the interconnectedness of this era of globalization, which makes the whole world seem like one huge village.

I understand the importance of preserving our traditions and values; but I also understand that some of these traditions no longer make sense because they simply do not work anymore. The new generation is enlightened and has seen more; it expects more. Is it such a stretch to expect marriage to be, at the very least, with someone you know well enough to be able to decide whether that person is compatible with you on a mental, spiritual, and emotional level? This is a person you are going to spend the rest of your life with, for God's sake! How can you decide if that person is the one you want to spend your life with just by talking with him/her on the phone? Am I the only one who thinks this is preposterous and an injustice to all of us young Qataris? Surely, I am not, but I suspect most of us settle for this arrangement, as it is the only way for traditional Qatari families to marry. Where else can you meet the opposite sex here? Everything else that involves contact with the opposite sex is looked down upon; it is taboo and we just have to accept that.

According to the Rand-Qatar Policy Institute, seventy-six percent of Qatari women who participated in their survey refuse to get employment in the private sector because it is a mixed gender environment (*The Peninsula*, 1 November 2008, page 1). Why, I ask, do we have to accept this as the norm without even so much as questioning it? I am all for preserving our traditions and culture but not when those traditions no longer make sense, either rationally or religiously. I have painted a picture that is perhaps guilty of generalization, but I contend that it is still based on what the majority of Qatari families are like. There are exceptions nowadays to these rules and in the spirit of integrity I mention those here; but it is important to emphasize that those are nevertheless exceptions to the norm.

We need to truly debate whether traditional arranged marriages merit being the only 'real' and acceptable way of getting married in Qatar, in this day and age. If not, what are the alternative ways that are considered to be still viable here (keep in mind, that according to the RQPI survey, seventy-six percent of women don't even want to work in a place that allows contact with the other sex)? We need a rational discussion in a public sphere between the young Qatari adults, to discuss these questions. That will be the first step towards truly adapting to and taking advantage of all that our ever-changing, ever-improving country is providing for us. I believe a dialogue will be the beginning of the process of designing a remedy that fixes at least one of the aspects in our society that escaped through the cracks of improvement.

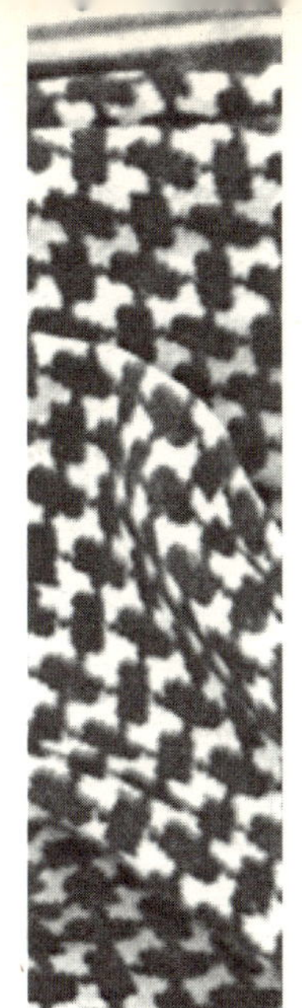

Modernization in Qatar

ALJOHARA YAQOUB AL JEFAIRI is an International Relations major at Qatar University. She has participated in a number of international conferences, as well as an educational trip to the United States. During these experiences as she meets people from other countries and religions, most of them, she finds, are surprised to discover that Qatari women have abilities and ambitions.

PHYSICALLY, QATAR IN 2008 is almost unrecognizable compared to Qatar in 1968, but in quality of life, social attitudes and political thinking it is also a different country. These social changes have come about partly as a consequence of the changes in physical infrastructure.

Following the first production of oil in 1949, and independence in 1971, Qatar developed the basic infrastructure of a modern state. Rumeillah Hospital was built in 1952; Doha Airport was constructed in 1963[1]. Official statistics show that in 1956 there were fourteen schools and 1,000 students in state education[2]. By 2006 and 2007 these numbers had increased to 278 schools and 11,249 students receiving education from the state[3]. Obviously, without construction of new schools, this increase would not have been possible.

With increased literacy came a greater awareness of social issues. The status of women in society, for example, became an issue as more women graduated from high school and university. There was social pressure to employ these girls and women in non-traditional jobs. Today, we find women engineers in Qatar Airways and women pilots in Gulf Helicopters and Qatar Airways[4]. How can we relate these changes to changes in infrastructure?

In 1968 the basic needs of the society were met in health and education. The buildings and services existed, but no attempt was made to upgrade facilities. As recently as 2000, some of the same schools still existed with ceiling fans for air-conditioning and many broken windows. These physical surroundings did not encourage students to love learning; indeed it seemed as if students were being sent to prison instead of school. Education was rarely discussed in the media and the Ministry of Education main building near the Corniche was as old and broken down as many of the schools. This was, perhaps, a sign of how unimportant the government felt education to be.

Recent developments in infrastructure have opened job opportunities which did not exist forty years ago. The gas industry has opened the door to many Qatari graduates including women. In 1968 less than twenty percent of the workforce was Qatari, and less than five percent was Qatari women. Today, in the oil and gas industries the percentage of Qataris has risen to fifty-five percent[5], and as industries grow that rely on oil or gas, such as chemical and fertilizer industries, this percentage of Qataris in employment continues to grow.

Engineers are also required to supervise the construction boom happening in Qatar now. Ashghal, the Public Works Authority, currently employs thirty-three percent Qataris[6]. With increased economic and construction activity, many other ministries and corporations are expanding their workforces and women are being employed in jobs previously held by foreign workers.

It is not only in government that the number of Qatari employees is increasing. In banks and private companies it is common to find Qataris working along with foreigners. If there was no infrastructure boom, it is unlikely that this would have happened. The trickle-down effect of increasing oil and gas revenues is making itself felt in many fields.

The most obvious example is in the development of higher education and the building of Education City. In most developed countries, a major city might have three, four or five universities, but with a population of millions. These universities are normally located in different parts of the city and have a tradition of competition rather than cooperation with each other. If we look at London, for example, we see that there are five major universities not close together and not able to allow their students to meet and collaborate[7]. In contrast, the vision of Qatar Foundation for Education and Science is distinct[8]. Here, the concept is to bring together, on one site, world-class universities in world-class buildings. Although the question is hypothetical, it is interesting to speculate whether these universities would have opened branches in Qatar without the assurance that the buildings and facilities provided by Qatar Foundation would be world class. The expenditure on building alone is an indicator of how serious Qatar Foundation is in trying to achieve its vision[9].

In addition, the teaching standard within these universities has also had an effect on education generally in Qatar. Qatar University has also undergone a process of reform. Standards of admission are higher, curricula have been revised, teaching is (mainly) in English and the possibility of making the university mixed sex has been discussed. Of course, it is possible that Qatar University would have made these reforms without the example of the universities based in Education City, but whether it would have aimed at raising standards to compete with these universities is doubtful, since for many years it was the only option for many students who wanted a university education. In other words, it had a monopoly and acted like most monopolies – too bad if you don't like the service!

The other area of education reform was in public primary and secondary education. The Supreme Education Council was established in 2002 to oversee the educational reform known as Education for a New Era, which actually started in 2001[10]. The short-term objective of this initiative is to build 'a modern world-class public school system' and in the long-term to 'prepare future generations to be productive members of Qatari society and the world at large'[11].

What is not noted is that in 2001, the government built forty-two new schools to replace older, run-down schools. The first independent schools were given some of these buildings. The new buildings make a new start in education possible. They are both symbolic and, at the same time, a practical demonstration of the desire of the state to improve education.

Another area of development and modernization is medical care and facilities. With oil money, the first public health care system was established in 1953. A public hospital was built and developed into Rumeillah Hospital. Doctors and nurses were recruited from the United Kingdom and a mass vaccination campaign against tuberculosis was set up; without oil money, this would have been impossible to fund[12]. Indeed, the first medical facility in Dukhan was established by the oil company. Before these medical facilities were built, people had to rely on folk medicine, wise women, and *mutawa* to try to cure illnesses. In 1972, with the rise in oil price caused by OPEC's decision to cut production[13], Qatar was able to build a new, modern hospital called Hamad Hospital. Currently this has been renamed Hamad Medical City and is building modern facilities in many specializations including IVF and cancer treatment. If oil was selling at ten dollars per barrel, as in 1996, would these facilities exist today?

Social life in Qatar has also changed with development.

Until the construction of shopping malls, it was very uncommon for groups of women or even for family groups to go to public places apart from the Corniche or a restaurant[14]. Now it is common for groups to go to a shopping mall as a social event. In other words, shopping is not the main activity. Both the mall and the people in the mall have become entertainment in themselves. Another area of entertainment that has proved popular with a growing number of Qataris is the cinema. Until about 1996, there were only two cinemas in Doha and they were not places families went to. Now, modern, comfortable, clean cinemas – offering a variety of entertainment for all ages and tastes – attract large numbers of people, especially on the weekend. This does not imply that traditional values have been lost, but, because the buildings and facilities exist, those who want to use them in ways that could not have existed sixty years ago have the opportunity to do so.

Food shopping has changed with the introduction of hypermarkets. Until 2001, supermarkets were not places many Qatari women frequented. As they mainly sold food, there was little incentive or attraction for Qatari women. People recall that food shopping was often done by men and the only places women went to shop were The Centre or the New Trade Gallery. Along with the spread of malls and hypermarkets came the introduction of international brands of clothes and food. A Starbucks does not seem out of place in a shopping mall, but would have seemed very strange in the old Souq Waqif. It is normal to see Qatari women in this type of coffee shop, while they could not have gone to a traditional small tea or coffee shop or shisha café. The opportunity only arose after the provision of the infrastructure[15].

The relaxing of social rules governing how women could be seen in public also carries over to driving. Now it is normal to see a woman wearing a *niqab* driving but if roads were not modern and not safer than they were even ten years ago, it is unlikely so many women would drive.

The development of the towers area of Doha has meant that many ministries and government departments have moved their offices there. The working conditions are clean, modern, and open. They are places where Qatari women can feel comfortable about working and the evidence is available to anyone who visits any of these buildings.

With the change in social attitudes noted above, there is has been a change in political life[16]. The new constitution and establishment of the Central Municipal Council have given Qataris the incentive to take part in public debates about issues that previously were only spoken about in private. Of course, it is not possible to claim that this is a direct result of modernization of the physical infrastructure, but there are links with the change in social attitudes brought about by the recent infrastructure development of the country. This is guided from above and encouraged by H.H. Sheikha Moza bint Nasser Al Misnad[17]. She has been the driving force behind Qatar Foundation, and she has also been a role model for many, especially women and girls, in Qatari society[18].

The modernization of information and information technology (IT) in Qatar has also played a key role in opening opportunities for Qatari citizens. The Internet allows everyone to access information from the world and to learn from the world. Jobs are available that did not exist sixty years ago. There are no barriers to women being as skilled as men in IT; this is not a 'traditional' field – there are no preconceived notions about 'men vs women' in this work. Qtel customer service staffs are now mainly women and deal professionally with customers' enquiries and problems.

Modernization can be viewed in two ways: the physical development of infrastructure and the change in social attitudes. It seems clear that the two are, in many respects, inter-connected. Physical development brings about social development. In the days before safe and cheap travel by air or road, the Hajj pilgrimage was a journey of a lifetime. Now, many people go for Omrah one or two times a year. In the same way, the development of the physical infrastructure of Qatar in the 1960s and 70s and recent developments over the past ten years have brought about significant changes in the lives of the citizens and residents of Qatar. In the first phase of development, the health and education of people changed dramatically as a result of modern facilities being built. In the second, and more recent, phase, social attitudes and mindsets have started to show signs of change. In both cases the changes are not reversible. It is not possible to return to 'the old ways'. It will be fascinating to see how and in what way future modernization changes Qatari society.

Notes

1 Gotting, Fay. *Healing Hands of Qatar.* Doha: Author and Publisher, 2006.
2 Ministry of Media, Qatar. Doha: Department of Publication: Ministry of Media, 1980.
3 Supreme Education Council. "Education in Schools of Qatar." Available from http://www.sec.gov.qa/EVI/SchoolingReport/Arabic-2006-07.pdf. Internet; accessed 2 May 2008.
4 Hassan, Zahra. "Woman pilot's bumpy ride." *The Peninsula.* Available from http://www.thepeninsulaqatar.com/Display_news.asp?section=Local_News &month=November2007&file=Local_News2007112035748.xml. Internet;, accessed 2 May 2008.
5 International Business Publications, *Qatar Business Law Handbook.* Washington DC, USA: Global Investment Centre , 2007.
6 Aldowaidi, Fathi. "The Neutral Commission to Examine the Grievances Career. Placement in "Ashghal"." *Newspaper Al Watan.* Available from http:// www.alwatan.com/data/20080113/innercontent.asp?val=local3_1. Internet; accessed 2 May 2008.
7 Directgov. "University and Higher Education." *Education and Learning.* Available from http://www.direct.gov.uk/en/EducationAndLearning/ UniversityAndHigherEducation/index.htm. Internet; accessed 2 May 2008.
8 Qatar Foundation. "Education City." Available from http://www.qf.edu.qa/ output/page301.asp. Internet; accessed 3 May 2008.
9 Yamani, Sarah. "al Nakhlah." The Fletcher School Online Journal for issues related to Southwest Asia and Islamic Civilization, (Spring 2006): 4.
10 Yamani, Sarah. "al Nakhlah." The Fletcher School Online Journal for issues related to Southwest Asia and Islamic Civilization, (Spring 2006): 3.
11 SEC. Supreme Educational Council of Qatar. Available from http://www. english.education.gov.qa/.Internet; accessed 3 May 2008.
12 Gotting, Fay. *Healing Hands of Qatar.* Doha: Author and Publisher, 2006.
13 WTRG Economics. "Oil Price History and Analysis." Crude Oil Prices. Available from http://www.wtrg.com/prices.htm. Internet; accessed 3 May 2008.
14 Steinkopff, "Cultural aspects of morbid fears in Qatari women." *Social Psychiatry and Psychiatric Epidemioligy.* 13 December 2004, 137-140.
15 The Peninsula. "Customers want first aid facility at shopping centres." Available from http://www.thepeninsulaqatar.com/Display_news.asp?section=local_ news&month=april2008&file=local_news200804202430.xml. Internet; accessed 3 May 2008.
16 Plascov, Avi . "Security in the Persian Gulf: Modernization, Political Development and Stability." *Jstor,* no. 98 (1983): 562-563.
17 Bahry, Louay and, Phebe, Marr. "Qatari Women: a New Generation of Leaders?" *Middle East Policy,* no. 12 (2005): 104-119.
18 Embassy of Qatar. «Women in Qatar.» Available from http://www. qatarembassy.net/women.asp. Internet; accessed 3 May 2008.Qatar.

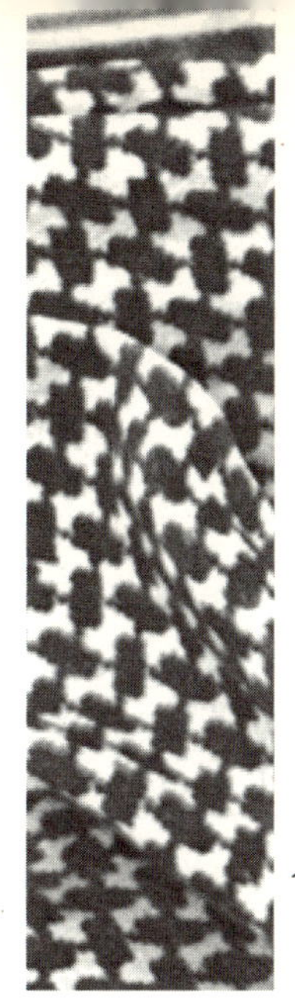

Qatar: Land of Opportunities

AL JAZZY ABDULLAH AL MARGAHI knows that when she is stressed, a pen and paper have always made her feel better. She expresses herself comfortably by pouring out her emotions and thoughts into writings. As a college student, she writes a lot of different kinds of essays, but finds cause and effect essays the most interesting. She believes that if you have a certain interest in something, you have to work hard to improve it and nourish it, and that is why she participated in this essay contest.

Currently, I am studying at Weill Cornell Medical College-Qatar, one of the best medical colleges in the world. Ten years ago, my doing this would have been considered a mere dream. However, the dramatic changes in education in Qatar were pivotal to my life and hopefully will be to my future as well.

One day when I was in the seventh grade, the principal came in to the middle of the classroom, interrupted the teacher, and called a few students' names. My name was on that list. I did not understand what was going on. The school distributed some papers among us and asked us to give them to our parents. In those papers, there was something mentioned about a new scientific school. My father was excited, since they chose only a few people to enrol in this school and they claimed it was one of the best schools in the country. The school was going to introduce a new approach to education in Qatar, and so they selected the best students to try this different style of learning. It wasn't until later that I felt really happy or appreciated this life-changing opportunity.

Everything happened fast. The days were flying by and the years were passing by, and I was walking along a new path in my life. Every day I learned new things that I never thought I would know until many years later. I was fortunate to have this kind of higher education; not all people had it at that time. When I entered high school, it was also a very different experience for me. School was not just about education and academic performance; we also had a lot of activities inside and outside the classroom. Education was all about balancing and consolidating our knowledge and gaining more information from other people, like the visitors from different schools, cultures, and countries. This kind of multi-cultural education helped us to be open-minded and not to restrict our thinking by boundaries.

Choosing a specialty and applying to college was the biggest step I have ever taken in my life. Having the best colleges in Qatar was a motivation for me to work harder in order to meet those colleges' requirements. I have always strived for greatness and being an average student was not something that I had in mind. I chose to enter the field of medicine and to work hard with the help of God in order to reach my goal.

After I began studying at the college, I had another surprise waiting for me. One time, I was sitting and doing my work after all my colleagues had left for home. My friend called me. She said, "You are on the list!" I wondered what she was talking about. What special list had my name on it?

She told me that I was one of the students who was going to be awarded for Excellence in Education by His Highness Shaikh Tamim Bin Hamad Al Thani. At that moment, I felt like all the hard work I had done was eventually going to be appreciated by others. The award gave me motivation to work even harder.

The ceremony happened a week later. We had to go early to rehearse. When I entered the hall, the place was dark, only sparsely lit with lights of different colours. People of all ages were there. One of the ceremony coordinators walked me to my seat, where I sat patiently waiting to rehearse before the ceremony began. The people in charge said that they would mention our names and we would have to walk fast to the stage. My name was the first on the list. At that moment I was shocked. I did not want to be the first person. I was very nervous. My parents arrived later that evening for the ceremony; they were happier than I was and very proud of my accomplishment.

When it was time for me to receive the award, I felt that my steps were heavy. I was nervous, and I could not move fast. However, when I reached the stage I felt more comfortable. I smiled, took my certificate, and had a picture taken with His Highness. When I got off the stage and sat in my chair, all of my friends started sending me messages, telling me how great I was. That moment was probably the best moment for me. To be successful and loved by other people was something that I always try to achieve. I have always liked to balance my work and social life, and that evening I felt I had achieved a perfect balance. When I went home, my brothers were waiting to congratulate me. That was one of the best days of my life.

I used to think that there are limits for our ambitions and dreams. Now I totally disagree with this point of view. We hear all the time that America is the land of opportunity, but now I certainly believe that Qatar is one, even more so. The changes in the last few years in Qatar's education have influenced many young people's lives for the better. As a British playwright once said, "You see things and you say, 'Why?' But I dream things that never were, and I say, 'Why not?'"

This is how I feel now.

You never know where you might end up or if your wildest dreams might eventually come true. You just have to believe in yourself and have faith in your dreams. I have full faith in mine.

What Does it Mean to Be a Qatari Woman?

NADYA AL AWAINATI was born in 1990 and was inspired to write this piece by the death of her grandmother. A student at Qatar University, her major is Industrial and Systems Engineering.

Originally appeared as "What Does it Mean to be a Woman in Qatar in 2008?"

QATAR IS A COUNTRY that was for a long time unknown. But seventy years ago, it started to become more popular and known in other countries around the world. This is because it became one of the richest countries, producing oil and natural gas. Qatar has undergone many changes that have affected the population and the government.

There are many differences between Qatar 2010 and Qatar 1940. Earlier, people's lives depended on fishing and pearl diving. Men used to sail the seas for many months. Women took care of the children, cooked and cleaned. They didn't make any particular contribution towards society, other than being good mothers.

My grandma, for example, was married at the age of fourteen. From then on she behaved as an adult woman, taking responsibility and making her own life in her own home. Her mother had taught her how to cook different types of complicated dishes when she was eight. Most of the time when she was growing up, she was the one who cooked lunch and prepared dinner. Sometimes when her mother worked to earn an income, selling different kinds of dates, she took care of her younger brothers and sisters. My grandma left school after grade three, because my grandfather decided to marry her. He was twenty-six years old. When she married him she wasn't mature enough to make the right decision – her parents planned her life without considering her opinion. During this time she was very happy. She believed that she was one of the happiest ladies at her age. She was the first one among her friends to marry. At that time, people believed that the more beautiful the lady, the earlier she was going to marry.

Nine years passed and my grandpa died. He left my grandma with six children. Only two of them were her own children, while all of the others were the responsibility of my grandpa. During that time, my grandma told me much later, women used to give birth in the home with no one to support them because the men were away sailing. Women were treated as super nannies for their men and children. Adding to that, men were the ones who controlled the family and women had no right to share their opinions with others.

My grandma suffered a lot with the six children, with difficulties in many different areas. She didn't know how to raise children, how to feed them, or how to educate them. She started to work in areas that were acceptable within society. She cooked dishes of food in order to sell them. After that, she worked as a seamstress for more than five years. During this time many men offered to marry her, but she refused all of them. Eventually she started to think logically and decided to marry her cousin in order to get support. He was a very kind man who loved all the children. He wasn't able to have children.

Years passed and Qatar developed more and more, as a result of the discovery of natural gas and petroleum. It became a very popular country. These developments affected the whole country in many different ways – lifestyle, culture, values, and education. But the biggest change was related to people's lifestyle. Education became an important part in every child's life. The government helped every child in Qatar to become well educated. Hospitals were built in order to ensure people had a healthy life, and the government became more aware of what was happening in the country. Men were no longer the only financial supporters for the family. Women were allowed to work in many different fields and to support the family. They were also given the right to vote and contribute to society. Some women started to have their own businesses and to be qualified in their fields.

Education was very important for both genders. Gender discrimination disappeared and the level of education became the only factor differentiating males and females. It became possible for women to earn high educational degrees from different countries around the world. At the beginning of the development of women's careers, they worked in a sheltered environment that didn't include men. Then people became more open-minded. As a result, women started to look for higher positions. They became engineers, doctors and politicians. They started to get more rights by fighting for themselves.

These changes created strong women who are confident enough to lead the next generation and to hold important responsibilities related to their own businesses. I think of the differences between my generation and my grandma's. I'm a seventeen-year-old lady, who is studying medicine at Weill Cornell Medical College in Qatar. I feel that I'm able to take responsibility for my life I have been through many challenges and obstacles that, with the help of my parents, have taught me to make the right decisions.

One of my biggest goals is to help society by being a diabetes consultant; I will help everyone who suffers from diabetes. My life differs from my grandma's. Her goal was to marry and give birth to many children to make her husband happy. She didn't think of how to help the society and how to use her talents. She depended on the man, as she believed that women couldn't take all the responsibilities without a male, a man who was going to support her financially.

Unlike my grandmother, my mother married when she finished high school. She married my dad and at the same time she was studying at university. A few months later she became pregnant. She faced a lot of troubles in her pregnancy, but she didn't delay any of her courses. My dad and mom helped themselves. After two years, my father decided to continue his studying abroad. So my mother held all the responsibilities on her shoulders. She was studying in the morning and raising us in the afternoon. She didn't give up; she tried to continue her studies, getting the highest degrees possible.

I think that Qatari women faced a lot of difficulties in developing themselves. One of the biggest obstacles is related to family and the Arabian culture. Most families were very strict and hard on their girls. Some families did not allow young women to study abroad alone. Other women could travel, but only with a close relative. The next obstacle was related to culture. Some families believed that if a woman started to work and study with males she will lose all her morals. Some husbands also believed this about their wives. They were very strict, not even allowing their wives to show their faces. Even though driving is allowed for women who are eighteen years old, many families refuse to allow their girls to drive a car. They think that Arab women in general are useless and can't contribute to society.

All in all, Qatari women are the best symbol of what Arab women face. They have had a lot of difficulties throughout their lives. But whatever the difficulty, they challenge themselves to do their best. If my grandma had started a family today, her life would have been so different.

Social Impact of Globalization on Qatar

NOFE KHALID AL SUWAIDI is a student at Carnegie Mellon in Qatar and a Business Administration major. She acknowledges that globalization is a positive force that benefits the state on various levels but understands there are challenges as well as benefits to this phenomenon. Qatar is growing at such a fast pace; Nofe would like to help her fellow citizens of Qatar examine the social impact of such growth in today's increasingly global world.

During the last few years, Qatar has taken globalization and modernization initiatives in search of greater economic benefits. As a result, the country has been rapidly changing, in terms of dress codes, standards of living, and lifestyles. At times the change could be beneficial to the economy and the political state of the country. In other instances, it could also strip a country of its sense of individuality and cultural heritage. Globalization and modernization in Qatar may have various negative social consequences – the deterioration of the Arabic language, the loss of cultural identity, and the undermining of Islamic religious values. In order to combat these problems, Qatar needs to make sure it preserves its cultural identity, language, and religious values.

Globalization and modernization have undeniably benefited Qatar in various aspects of society. They have given Qatar access to world-class education, higher standards of living, and a greater sense of cultural awareness and social equality. Qatar has adopted the Education City project, in which it has invited a collection of prestigious American universities to open up branches here in Doha. Some of these universities include Carnegie Mellon University, the Georgetown School of Foreign Service, Texas A&M University, Virginia Commonwealth University School for the Arts, and Weill Cornell Medical College. Qatar has invested in education reform with the aim of creating an academically stronger Qatari youth.

In addition, globalization has developed the economic and social state in Qatar. Today Qatar is one of the fastest-growing economies in the world with one of the highest per capita incomes. Moreover, Qatar has created greater cultural awareness and global citizenship as a result of globalization. Cultural awareness is exercised as it is exposed to more foreign influences through education, media, and free trade. At the same time, global citizenship is exercised through the creation of various humanitarian relief efforts organizations such as Reach Out to Asia, Qatar Red Crescent, and Qatar Charity. Furthermore, increasingly groups within society are being granted greater rights. For example, women have been granted the right to vote.

Despite the various benefits, globalization and modernization may strip Qatar of its cultural identity and sense of individuality. Ramzy Baroud, author of an article called 'Weathering the Globalization Storm' (*Counterpunch*, 17 February 2006) addresses this by claiming that globalization strips Third World countries of their sense of cultural identity. The author argues that Qatar has abandoned the traditional villages in favour of Western-style projects. In addition, Baroud points out that Qatar has neglected its cultural initiative for the sake of globalization and economic welfare. As a Qatari citizen, I believe that it is in fact true that Qatar has somewhat ignored the old architectural sites and allowed them to perish.

For the purposes of this research, I interviewed Lulwah Hamad Al Thani, daughter of the Emir of the state of Qatar, about the effects of globalization on Qatar. She comments, "It disturbs me to see some individuals adopting a complete Western style of life and abandoning our social heritage." She believes that as a result of globalization some Qatari nationals abandon their cultural identity in search of a 'Western' way of being. In effect, adopting a Western way of life dilutes the Qatari identity and cultural heritage to a degree that it may be neglected and lost.

Moreover, globalization in Qatar creates the dilemma of undermining Arabic, the prominent language within the region. The importance of the Arabic language and the practice of the language itself are decreasing, as a result of globalization and the extensive use of English as the international language of business and higher education. A survey of twenty CMU-Q students was conducted to find out what people thought of the influence of globalization and modernization on Qatar. The survey showed that seventy-five percent believed that the number of Arabic speakers would decline in Qatar as a result of globalization. In comparison, Lulwah Al Thani asserts, "I think our language will always be preserved simply because it is the language of the Quran."

She states that the deterioration of the Arabic language is not a problem. She believes that there are measures that should be taken to make sure that the Arabic language does not lose its importance and dominance within the region. However, it is undeniable that Arabic has been abandoned as the primary language of education. Furthermore, we find that today's Qatari youth value English more than they value the Arabic language, as a result of the increasing number of English-medium schools and American-style universities in Qatar. Consequently, globalization and modernization could have negative influences on the Islamic core values in Qatar.

Through media, free trade, and education, Islamic values may be undermined as a result of cultural integration. Teenagers are allowed access to media content that is vulgar and profane. This content threatens the strict Islamic values that the state of Qatar has managed to hold onto since its founding. In addition, through free trade, products such as alcohol, which is considered a sin, are being introduced into the Qatari market. Moreover, higher education in the form of English-medium schools and American universities are constantly pushing the envelope when it comes to teaching. Qatar has employed the 'hands off' approach in terms of the teachings given in the American universities. This has developed today's youth into intellectual individuals with high levels of expertise in multiple fields. However, this has also introduced religion-threatening courses such as 'The Problem of God', which is currently given to students studying at the Georgetown School of Foreign Service. The course consists of teachings about a variety of religions and belief systems. The course challenges the faiths and religious values of the Qatari and Arab nationals in the country (www.diverseeducation.com/artman/publish/article_5931.shtml). In spite of this, introducing challenging courses provides students with intellectual and individual thinking skills – skills that are needed to create higher thinking abilities.

In order to combat these potential threats to Qatari culture and society, the state of Qatar and the nationals of Qatar need to identify that there is a problem that needs to be tackled. First of all, Qatar has to develop methods to preserve the cultural identity of Qatar, its Islamic values and its local language. All of this can be achieved through educating the public. To begin with, parents and educators need to identify with the Qatari identity. The Qatari identity in the past was a combination of Gulf-based traditions and Islamic values.

Today, the identity has reshaped itself into a form where Qatari nationals have the same basic ideals and values at the core but with a greater sense of acceptance and awareness of other cultures. In order to preserve the primary ideals and values of the Qatari identity, schools must make sure that they embed in the students the ideals and history of the state of Qatar at the primary and secondary levels. Educators must also make sure to create a sense of pride in the Qatari identity and a sense of distinctness to such a degree that if globalization or any other global force takes place in Qatar it will not be able to strip the country of its cultural identity.

Lulwah Al Thani believes, "We should be careful and preserve our basic ideals and religion because those two things must never be compromised. We should accept globalization only to the extent that our basic identity is not at stake." (Al Thani, Lulwah, personal communication, 2007)

For example, Qatar could host national celebrations as an opportunity to maintain the cultural identity of the country. In addition, Qatar could also form cultural societies or organizations that operate with the sole purpose of educating the public about Qatari identity and its importance. With the fast growth rate of Qatar's economy, it was inevitable that Qatar's identity would be altered and reshaped to be more accepting and inclusive of other cultures. However, Qatar must make sure that its identity does not lose its primary ideals; it should only become more accepting of other cultural identities.

To maintain the high importance of the Arabic language, Qatar has to keep an attentive eye on the education its students are receiving. Qatar has to make sure that the schools and parents are teaching Arabic as a core subject with the same importance, if not more, than any secondary languages. Lulwah Al Thani believes that parents should have a proactive role in the lives of their children to make sure that Arabic is exercised and learned. In addition, the Qatari education system must also maintain the Islamic teachings at all levels of study especially during the growth stages between primary and secondary school. In addition, the education system in Qatar should be reformed to include Arabic in all subjects. English should not be the only prominent language in all but Islamic studies. Arabic should be included in the core subjects as well.

In conclusion, I have identified that globalization has various negative social effects on Qatar that we, as Qataris, have to tackle. We first have to highlight what these negative social impacts are: loss of cultural identity, undermining of the Arabic language, and weakening of Islamic values and ideals. To overcome the consequences of globalization, the state of Qatar needs to educate tomorrow's youth and the parents and teachers of tomorrow's youth on the importance of the Qatari identity, the Arabic language, and Islamic values. Most importantly, Qatar has to embed a sense of pride and joy into all of its citizens towards everything to do with Qatar. With such feelings and passion towards the country, Qataris would be able to withstand the forces of globalization. Qatar's identity, religious values, and local language could remain intact.

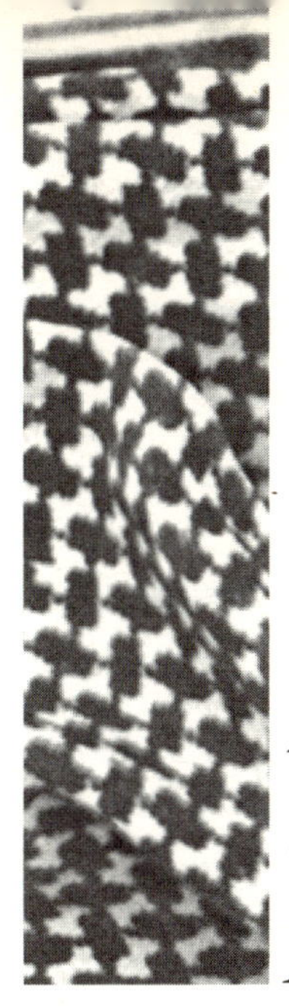

Qatar: Through the Eyes of Essa Abdullrahman Al Mannai

NOORA AL MANNAI is a graduate of the International Baccalaureate program at Qatar Academy and an aspiring writer. She is very interested in literature and history, particularly the history of the Middle East. She feels blessed to be part of Qatar's new educated generation and comes from a large family where she is the youngest girl with four older brothers. Her status in her family means she constantly fights to be recognized; thus she is constantly trying to prove herself. She hopes one day to be able to display her full potential positively through her writing in her country. She is studying International Affairs at Georgetown University.

The grains of my country's sand may scar the palms of my hands but I will never let them go.

THESE WERE THE WORDS of the patriotic Qatari national, Essa Abdullrahman Al Mannai, describing his love for Qatar. Essa Al Mannai is a prominent businessman in the country and he has lived here the full fifty years of his life. He has witnessed first-hand the dramatic change that has occurred in this country – economically, culturally, educationally, socially, and politically. For this essay, I interviewed Essa Al Mannai, my father.

The change in Qatar's economy has been great and this has had a huge impact on the way people live today – their morals, beliefs, relationships with one another, and, most importantly, their way of life. In the past, "ladies would do all the cleaning", Essa Al Mannai says, and therefore the role of women was limited to cleaning the house. This was the result of extended-family housing, where the family all lived together and would provide financial support for members of the same household; women did not need to work outside the home then. They were taken care of. With the boom to the economy, small families began separating away from and no longer living with the entire family, as they could now stand on their own two feet. This independence caused family relationships to weaken, as each member was no longer in dire need of the other. Men then needed to allow their wives to work, Mr Al Mannai explained during our interview.

The first jobs women could have were simple. They were not given the opportunity to work where they wished. Even if they were just as capable or even more capable than men, they were restricted to teaching and nursing. Only recently has women's role in Qatar flourished and shown prominent progress. Now Qatari women can begin to compete with accomplished women in other societies. In order for Qatar to develop it needed to be more open and to allow an opportunity for women to prove themselves, according to Mr Al Mannai.

Sheikha Moza has of course played a leading role in Qatar's social change as she fights for the rights of education. By creating Qatar Foundation, she has made sure that Qatari men and women can study together in a new positive environment. The Foundation is of the highest calibre and is devoted to promoting education and offering the highest standards in all of Qatar.

Another significant change is the promotion of education itself. Today there are many students willing to learn; families today encourage learning. Before the rise of the economy, recalls Mr Al Mannai, students "... would go camping in the desert in Qatar. So all of a sudden in December-January we would see half of the students in the classroom absent; even some of the administrators and teachers would be absent!" Parents used to take their children on these trips, expressing their negligence towards education.

With the rise of oil revenues, the government tried to promote education by "giving allowances to students even in elementary school," recalls Mr Al Mannai. He also says that in Qatar back in the 1950s there were "few schools and also few students". However the earlier negligence and underestimation of the importance of education has been remedied within the Qatari culture by the availability of competitive scholarships and the launch of excellent universities.

On the other hand, the change in Qatar environmentally, according to Mr Al Mannai, is also great. It is one of the negative changes that has come along with the many positive changes he has witnessed. Mr Al Mannai remembers that the sea was "not polluted. It was clear and the beaches off the coast were very beautiful. The water was clean and the fish were abundant, so we never thought that there could ever be an environmental problem." The discovery of gas has caused companies to process these natural resources and this affects the environment negatively. As a result, the sea in Qatar today is much more polluted than it was only twenty or thirty years ago.

Change in Qatar has arrived. It started slowly. But as Qatari families became more educated and learned about the benefits of change, they accepted it, causing the last five or six years in Qatar to be of most significance, economically, educationally, socially, and even politically. Qatar's relationship with America is probably the most mutually beneficial compared with other Arab countries. The alliance, according to Mr Al Mannai, who refers to himself as "patriotic", is "a sovereign decision for Qatar to take and I think there is a mutual agreement where the Americans and Qataris have a mutual understanding of how to conduct their operations and consider each other's interests." Qatar is a small country and he believes, in order for it to prove itself, it needs a strong relationship with the world's super power.

The greatest political change in Qatar was in 1997 when Shaikh Hamad bin Khalifa overthrew his father. "I don't consider it a coup," says Mr Al Mannai. "Shaikh Hamad was the heir apparent and he was second in line for rule in

Qatar, feeling the country required younger blood and younger thinking. He decided to take over and rule because he had more vision of how to introduce positive change to the country."

Therefore the change of rulers has caused a substantial change in the country, change that was welcomed by most of the people. One of the most significant changes, which came with Shaikh Hamad's ruling, was the development of roads, the urban environment, and, most importantly, the development of civil laws, like the establishment of a constitution.

To conclude, Qatar has changed tremendously over the past fifty years – first with the discovery of oil, and then with the change of rule in 1997. The government focused on promoting positive change, like encouraging the role of women in society, developing the country's infrastructure, and building the country's education systems. However with this immense positive change came negative changes, which were not accounted for, like environmental problems from pollution and the public's views becoming more materialistic. But as Essa Al Mannai notes, "With every change there is a drawback."